Midnight Scoundrel

A Soulmark Series

Rebecca Main

DEDICATION

To my family and loved ones, thank you for supporting me. A special thanks to Anne, Christy, Felicia, Kim, and, of course, **Bear**. You are all wonderful!

TABLE OF CONTENTS

CHAPTER 1

Two days prior

- Ryatt -

The bar is a dump. A skim of the narrow landscape is all that's needed to confirm the fact. My nose wrinkles at the smell of stale, days-old alcohol. The likes of which seeped into the walls decades ago, along with the patrons. It is not a place to meet new people. Nor to gather with friends and lament your day's end. Here the patrons sit widely apart, each oozing their declarations of "fuck off" with slumped shoulders and threatening scowls.

It suits my needs exactly, for I've no wish to be bothered. I stop mid-step when my inspection is interrupted by a golden beauty sulking at the dingy bar.

She's wearing one of those off-the-shoulder dresses that seem to be all the rage this summer. Her hair, half up, sits high atop her head in one of those messy little buns with glimpses of silver dripping from her ears. And then there is her skin. Tan and healthy—

1

glowing. She is like an oasis in this desert dump, pining away over several empty shot glasses and a cell phone. The beauty casts a wary glance over her shoulder as the door slams shut behind me. Her blue eyes widen from afar, her lips falling into a gentle "O" before she sends me a determined frown. It's a much gentler "fuck off" than all the others I receive. It's quite adorable really. Certainly not enough to stop me.

I send her a grin that falls somewhere between lascivious and mischievous and saunter forward.

"What's a nice girl like you doing in a bar like this?" I ask, making sure my voice is a pleasant, husky hum as I seat myself next to this golden goddess. The duffle bag I carry is set gingerly underneath the barstool I chose.

"How original," she responds tartly. Disdain evident. Her eyes flicker toward me curiously, to run the length of my body, lingering a tad too long to be respectable. I make sure to keep myself poised under her scrutiny, muscles flexing minutely under it. She scoffs belatedly, a blush rising to her cheeks as if she is aware of her *faux pas*. A pleased smile ventures onto my lips when she turns her attention to the bartender. Fingers fluttering away to signal him. "Another, José."

"I'll have whatever the lady is having, but make it a double." She stiffens slightly, and I watch in interest as she attempts to ignore me. She's certain to have a difficult time of it.

I inhale. She is by far the prettiest thing I've seen in miles, and she smells of a tangle of emotions: fear, adrenaline, and the faintest trace of arousal. All blended between hints of lilac and lavender perfume. Of course, there is a touch of grief mingled in between, but it's the same as every other poor sap in this godforsaken bar. She casts another sidelong glance my way as the tequila is set in front of us. Will she take the bait?

"Cheers," she chirps after a moment's hesitation. Her smile is a brittle thing as she thrusts her shoulders back and swirls her creaking stool toward me. The liquid is down her throat before I can even reach my glass. If I didn't know better, I'd say she was some supernatural creature with her speed and grace, but her scent is completely human. I let out an amused chuckle before knocking back mine.

"Going somewhere, sweetheart?"

I let my eyes flick toward the pale pink suitcase near her feet, but hers do not follow as I expect. A delicate chime trills from her phone and with a sigh, she gives the electronic her attention. Her brow scrunches together, lips pursing as she furiously types a response. By the time she has finished, I have already signaled José for another round. When the drinks are set down, she gives another gentle scoff and flips her hair over her shoulder.

"Gee, thanks." But there is nothing sweet about the way her rosy lips curl into such a saccharine smile. Playing hard to get? No problem.

"Let me guess," I lean closer, a devious and knowing smirk in place. "You just broke up with your boyfriend. This was your first big trip together, and

3

you caught him with someone else. One of those dark-haired beauties around these parts. Now you're making the trek back home, all by your lonesome, pissed off and upset that you wasted your time and money on a vacation that ended in heartbreak. Am I close?"

She swallows, her eyes widening and her heartbeat ticking up just a fraction. Her surprise is palpable, so I soften just a tad and reach for the tequila.

"Something like that," she finally mutters.

"I've always preferred the fairer types," I tell her. The scoff I earn is mixed with a furtive laugh, one she is quick to mask behind a cough. *Got you.* "Kyle," I lie, lifting the shot glass in a peace offering. Her icy gaze melts and shifts to the remaining shot glass.

"Fuck it," she mumbles under her breath, snatching up the shot glass and clinking it against mine. We down it as one and politely ignore each other's grimaces as the amber liquor burns its way down. "Mary," she offers. My sights narrow at the way her voice goes a little high at the end, my hearing picking up the way her heart skips a beat. She raises an eyebrow in challenge, but I only chuckle. Why not play this little game of lies and see where it takes us?

"Tell me all about your troubles, sweet Mary," I coo. She rolls her eyes, the hint of a smile gracing her lips.

"I'm not nearly drunk enough," Mary confesses coyly. I'm about to respond when one of her legs drags itself up and across the other. Her dress, already so short, hikes up another perilous inch to reveal more sun-kissed skin. I let my gaze enjoy the newly revealed flesh for a moment before capturing her eyes with mine. I put on a wolfish grin and enjoy the way she replies in kind with her own knowing smirk. Let the games begin.

+++

Mary is a recent graduate from the Art Institute of California in San Francisco. She waxes on about the likes of Friedrich and Turner. How the dark and gloomy Romanticism speaks to her soul.

I am a nomad. Traveling South American with all that's left to my name in the bag at my feet. I tell her how I revel in the nights spent under the stars and my daring treks across the scorched and barren earth, but I'm always hungering for something more.

She has stopped taking her shots in one toss, preferring to sip on the molten elixir instead. Her baby blue eyes turn to steely storms, as the hours tick on. When I tease at her inability to keep up, she reminds me that she has been sitting at this desolate bar much longer than I. And that she is always able to keep up.

Somewhere around shot 11 or 12, I slip and call her beautiful. It brings the most delicious blush to her cheeks. Though she eyes me speculatively from beneath her long lashes, she does not rebuff my compliment. A few more shots taken, and she proclaims she's never been with a real man. One who knows how to take care of a woman, or himself, for that matter. I confess that I've never been in love. That no woman has been able to tame my wild heart. Her eyes widen.

When I return from the bathroom—a literal shit hole—Mary is collecting her things and attempting to finish off a bottle of water she's pulled from her purse. She wiggles it enticingly in front of me, only a quarter of the bottle left. I take it and sit down with a huff, finishing the warm water in two long drags.

"You're leaving?" I mumble. The bathroom mirror has proven my eyes are just as glazed as hers, if not more. They lose their hunter's sharpness, but I know in my gut this night has already been sealed.

"I leave tomorrow on an early flight," she explains clumsily, her heartbeat picking up. "I should really go get some sleep while I can."

I nod knowingly, but reach out and grab her wrist before she can take a step. "Where are you staying?"

"At a motel nearby," she whispers, letting the silence grow between us as she leans her body ever so slightly toward me.

A twinkle sparkles behind my misty blue eyes. "Me too."

+++

Our bags are left carelessly near the door of her motel room as the door slams shut behind us. I let her press my body against the cool metal. I savor the way her luscious curves sink into me as she attacks my mouth. I groan into the kiss, enthused with her eager attentions, and kiss back just as zealously. It has been rough these past few weeks trying to track down the other half of the Crystal of Dan Furth, but I did it. Now our alliance with the Trinity Coven will be cemented, and our lands guaranteed protection. I deserve a reward. One night of wicked splendor spent with this little lost lamb before going home victorious to my pack.

Her nails rake a path down my chest and tug at the belt wrapped around my waist.

"Bed," she whispers hotly against my lips. I nod, driving forward until we land in a heap atop the questionable blanket. The bed lets out a long groan of protest as we work our way toward the middle.

"You. Are. Glorious." I punctuate each word with a searing kiss. She lets out a breathy laugh. "And so fucking soft." I nuzzle the warm flesh of her neck, breathing in the heavy scent of adrenaline and arousal wafting from her skin. It is more obvious to me now that I am in far worse shape than she is, as her deft fingers work magic on my body. She pulls back, out of breath and observes me through lust-filled eyes. A beat later, she reaches toward the nightstand near her head to snatch a water bottle. She downs the small amount of water left in it before tossing it to the ground with a satisfied sigh.

"You should drink more water," she tells me matter-of-factly, tossing a look to the other half-empty bottle still on the nightstand. "I don't want you losing steam halfway because you're dehy—" I roll my eyes but do as she says, seizing the bottle on my second attempt and finishing it off in messy gulps.

"Good boy," she teases before flipping me onto my back. I let out a wry laugh, pushing aside the way my head swims at the motion and placing my hands on her hips to steady myself. If she prefers to take control—scorn that ex-boyfriend of hers—so be it. The view from the bottom is one of my favorites.

Mary locks eyes with me and grinds her hips down. Immediately our stunted moans fill the room. She is stunning, her hair mussed and framing her face. Her lips part and eyes darken to a fever pitch. When she rolls her hips again, she lets her fingers fist into the fabric of my Henley, moaning low in her throat at the coarse friction. Then my shirt is being pulled away from my body to explore the expanse of my chest and abs. When her hands tease lower, I watch her through heavy-lidded eyes. She makes her descent slowly, caressing my neck, then chest with her soft lips.

A wave of dizziness stirs in my head at the sensation. An almost purr-like noise escapes as her teeth dare to nip at the taut muscles of my pectorals. I let my hands wander the length of her thighs. Venturing higher and higher until her secret is discovered. I let out a sound of deep longing and look at her with newfound interest.

"You are full of surprises, little lamb," I hiss, fingers meeting only warm skin. There is nothing between her and me, except my jeans. She gives a saucy smile and slaps away my hand. "Tease," I mumble, stretching my arms languidly back and allowing her to do as she pleases. She sinks lower, leaving wet, open-mouth kisses all the way down south of my navel. Nip. Kiss. A swirl of the tongue and down one inch more.

"What's the rush?" she whispers as she undoes my belt and jeans, then jerks them down. I cannot contain my animalistic growl, the wolf inside me howling in anticipation. It is unusually riled, but then again, I have not indulged in skin this sweet in weeks. We are both starved. I attempt to lean up on my elbows but find myself suddenly extremely fatigued. I needed more water.

"Water," I beg, voice hoarse as I look around the nightstand, then to her. My little vixen. She's situated comfortably between my thighs, licking her lips as she stares down my cock.

"Impressive," Mary says, tongue flicking out to trace its head and ignoring my plea. I grit my teeth and inhale deeply through my nose. Screw the water then. My hand reaches down to cup the back of her neck and guide her lips around my aching cock when the most startling sensation overcomes me. With a strangled gasp, my hips lurch upward and I enter the warmth of her mouth. She releases a moan, eyes wide and a bit unsure as they look up at me.

Fuck.

The world around me bends and snaps. It shifts. A monumental movement suddenly centers my whole being around this little slip of a thing sucking so tightly on me now. My fingers tighten and urge her forward. To take me deeper as the passion unfurls

9

inside me like some raging bull. No prior experience can possibly compare to this moment. This revelation.

Without a doubt, hidden behind her luxurious locks is a soulmark to match my own. There is no other explanation for this sudden euphoria, and the wolf inside of me growls its sound agreement. To be sure, my fingers must lie on three lines, stacked neatly atop each other. The matching mark reminiscent of the Greek letter *xi.* She lets out another softer moan, eyes fluttering closed. And then her tongue is moving, a gentle sweeping caress along the underside of my shaft. I must taper back the vicious snarl curling at the rear of my throat as my head falls back from the pure ecstasy of her touch. She draws herself upward slowly. Her lips sealed tightly around me as she drags out the sensation. Just as her lips seek to release me, my hips chase after her of their own accord. A flex of my fingers, and she stalls to accommodate my pursuit. I bow forward, trembling to keep from thrusting too deeply and hitting the back of her throat.

"*Christ.*" A heavy pant falls from my lips as stars erupt behind closed eyes. Around me. Inside me. There is nothing but Mary and her warm embrace.

She grabs my wrist, urging my hand to release its hold. I relax my grip, fingers lingering as I pull back my hips. Her hand becomes more insistent. Then a sudden striking fear takes hold of my heart. I cannot miss what will most likely be my only opportunity to seal the soulmark. My fingers tighten for a fleeting second.

"Let it be known that thee are found," comes my

ragged whisper, "and my soul awakened. The stars incline us, my love, and so we are sealed." I gasp at the sudden all-encompassing glory that hits me. Reveling in the sound of her muffled moans around my cock. The vibrations entice my hips to press onward once more in short jerking movements to fuck her mouth.

"Fucking hell," I grunt as my load spills unexpectedly inside her. She pulls away, much to my dismay, somehow finding the strength to push away my hand and remove those succulent lips.

"What the fuck," she hisses, eyes wide and fully dilated. She wipes away the vestiges of my release from her face, an angry scowl marring her beautiful features. "What the fuck was that?" Her hand races to the back of her neck as she slips off the bed. Away from me.

"I can explain," I mutter, trying and failing to roll onto my side and go after her. My limbs lack their usual strength and dexterity.

"Listen," she calls from the bathroom. "I know guys get into the whole, 'choke on this, bitch' stuff, but I need a little warning before getting into that kind of shit, okay? You can't just... do that and not fucking warn a girl. Not cool." The sink turns on full blast, and I hear rather than see her splashing water over her face.

"What's your name?" I ask, unperturbed by her anger. I'll make up for it later, but first I need to know her real name.

"Mary," she snaps, walking up to the bed with her

11

hands on her hips. "Asshole."

"Not Mary," I correct, words slurring. "Your real name."

The smile she shares with me is tight. Her eyes sparkling vindictively down at me. A slow comprehension fills me with dread. She is most certainly not as drunk as I am. I suddenly wonder if she ever was.

"Guilty as charged," she says with a smirk. "How are you feeling, champ?"

I swallow, my eyes narrowing even though wave after wave of paralyzing weightlessness hits me. "What have you done?" Comes my rasping plea.

"Don't worry, *Kyle*. This will all be over in three... two..."

My eyes fall closed against my will as the strength in my body leaves me completely. I succumb to darkness. Her radiant figure a fixture in my mind's eye as I drift away into the sea of shadows that is my mind.

+++

Present Day

"And when I woke up, she was gone. Along with the crystal," I tell them with a lamenting cringe, waiting for the outburst that is sure to come. Xander stands stock still, the little vein near his left temple jutting out. And dear little Zoelle is both flushed and flustered. Perhaps I went a tad too much into detail. I

12

shoot her a knowing smirk, and her blush deepens.

"The crystal is gone?" Xander asks once more.

I swallow, feeling the weight of disappointment heavy in his words, and hold back another cringe. Soon enough my feigned composure crumbles under it, leaving a swell of regret and shame to rise as I am forced to acknowledge my failure. To know I have let down my alpha and caused him displeasure curls my stomach. Except, I didn't just let down my alpha with my dalliance, but my pack and our allies as well. My head tips to the side with a whine as his displeasure continues to relay itself through the pack bonds.

"It's all right, Ryatt," Zoelle assures me, her hand coming to rest on my shoulder. "We'll figure something out. Right, Xander?"

There is a tense pause. I dare not look my brother in the eye, remaining in my submissive stance and exposing my neck further to appease him. Finally— finally—he lets out a long-suffering sigh and that pressure in my heart, the one cinching it shut like an iron fist, lessens and releases. Another warm hand finds my shoulder. This one larger. Stronger. Better.

"We'll figure something out, brother," he reassures me. I nod and take a deep breath. Then another.

"On the upside," I say, slipping back into a more relaxed stance, eyes lifting meekly to meet theirs. "I found my soulmark." My lips twitch upward, a feeling of unmistakable joy spiriting through me. Zoelle peeks a quick glance at her fiancé, dazzling him with a brilliant smile and burst of gleeful laughter. He melts. His shoulders fall back and eyes light up for his soulmark. The dolt.

"But you don't even know her real name," Zoelle cries in distress, effectively ruining the moment. I roll my eyes at her dramatics.

"*Au contraire*, soon-to-be-sister. I do."

Their eyebrows rise in unison. "You do?"

"But of course. I've been hard at work the past day or so getting my fingers into this and that. Her real name is Quinn Montgomery."

"How did you find out so fast?" Zoelle asks, her head tipping curiously to the side. Xander merely rolls his eyes.

"I have a multitude of talents," I inform her graciously, "as you well know, and one of them just so happens to be 'hacker extraordinaire.' Anything can be found on the internet these days if you know how to look."

"What else do you know?" Xander asks. The continued retreat of his hostility allows me room to breathe without that strange pressure around my heart.

"She's twenty-two."

"Young, even for you," Zoelle chimes in cheekily.

"An orphan. No family to speak of: mother dead, father out of the picture. From ages eleven to fifteen, she was in the state system until, seemingly, falling off the grid," I tell them without pause. My mind fills in the blanks I leave out. Father *never* in the picture. The mother died of an overdose only to be found by little Quinn after she returned from school one chilly autumn day. Subsequently, she was tossed from foster home to group home time after time until the therapy she found in painting and sketching just wasn't cutting it anymore. She turned to crime, using her artistic abilities to dabble in forgeries and other petty thefts until one day she found herself playing in the big leagues. Too bad she had yet to learn how to cover her tracks. It's not easy to hide from a wolf, but hiding from an Adolphus is a different matter altogether.

"Sounds like you've been busy," Xander says.

"I have."

"I assume you have a plan," he continues, the corner of his lip ticking upward as I give him a somewhat bashful smile. A chuckle escapes my lips. The one that has been fine-tuned to give my audience pause. Xander raises a brow. Zoelle sends me an unsure smile.

"I have something in mind."

CHAPTER 2
- Quinn -

There's something so freeing about pretending to be someone you're not. Especially when that someone has no qualms spending a cool two grand on a pair of Christian Louboutin, Fabiola Over the Knee Boots. It hardly mattered that said boots had yet to be properly broken in and were forming major blisters on both pinky toes. *Nope.* Such were the daily trials and tribulations of my character's day: *Colette Winters.*

Denver, Colorado didn't quite fit the vibe of the character I donned—California rich girl—but she would do. She was certainly one of my favorite personas to take on, if not solely because of her wardrobe. I was waiting at The Brown Palace for my current employer to show up. He was late, but with the payout from my most recent job, I didn't care. Not that much anyway. After all, an order of Veuve Clicquot for Two had been placed immediately upon my arrival. So although his timing wasn't to be applauded, his taste in dining most certainly was. I assumed the heavy rain thundering down outside had a strong play in his lack of punctuality. Downtown traffic was excruciating because of it.

I give a cursory look over the other occupants of the tea room on this dreary Monday afternoon. Lots of old biddies with their daughters and granddaughters. Not a man in sight, save for the waiters who come by with their charming, youthful smiles, hoping to snag a hefty tip. I barely bat an eyelash when my own comes around to deliver the champagne.

I heave an unladylike sigh once he is out of hearing range. He's cute and kind of charming, but not like a certain somebody had been. The melancholy I have been fighting for the better part of two days rears its ugly head again. Where the damnable thing has come from I have no idea. Yet it lingers and grows as the days tick by. The thought that my despondency could stem from a certain raven-haired man does nothing to appease my rare mood. Especially when a thorough review of said feelings seems to lead back to him.

It wasn't guilt I was feeling. Kyle—or whatever his real name was—was just another pretty face, with a pretty piece of property somebody else wanted. Simple as that.

I had done it a dozen times before. The dingy bar. The sob story. The spiked water. Stumbling back to the decoy bedroom, only to tuck them in and take their shit. Hook, line, and sinker. Every. Single. Time. My targets could hardly make it to the bed before the

Rohypnol started to kick in. Kyle had lasted a remarkably long time, all things considered. It was somewhat impressive actually. I take a delicate sip of champagne to hide the flush that creeps up onto my cheeks as I think of just how long he lasted.

That particular portion of my plan had not gone as I had envisioned. Though that's not to say it went terribly. It was quite the opposite. Another blush dares to blaze across my cheeks as thoughts of his heated moans and the dizzying sensation of his touch collect at the forefront of my mind. How was it even possible to feel such a torrent of emotions from one intimate act? And yet the feel of his hand cradling my neck while I took him inside my mouth was an unbelievably pleasurable experience. Never before had I felt the building of such pleasure that I was almost torn from reality. I hadn't minded going down on him one bit, and that in itself was even more unbelievable.

My eyes flick towards the second glass of Veuve that is placed before an empty seat. I long to reach out and down it, but that's hardly how this native Californian would act. Not Colette Winters, I think.

So instead I set my flute down and scan the sea of plumed hats and demurely set shoulders for my waiter. I offer him a small smirk when I catch him making his way over with a tea tray filled with scones, pastries, and those little finger sandwiches I just love.

"Thank you," I say softly once he has set down the tray and refilled my glass. I refuse the tea that comes with the service. My dietary needs fulfilled with all that is already offered: sweets and champagne.

"Ms. Montgomery."

My second glass stalls at my bottom lip as my eyes flick sideways. Mr. Vrana stares down at me with familiar intensity, his words sharp as crystal. I straighten my spine and set down my glass. He waves off my attempt to stand and seats himself.

"Please, don't stop on my account," he muses, draping a napkin over his lap and looking over the presentation before him. He places a scone on his plate and lifts his glass of champagne, easing it forward in a gentle slant towards me. "I do believe congratulations are in order."

I plaster a large smile on my face. "All in a night's work," I assure him smoothly, picking my glass back up and sipping from it tentatively. We share a measured look over the fine china before I flit my gaze towards the third chair at our small table. On it sits a small Prada bag, gleaming white and proudly stamped. Its insides carry very precious cargo.

"For me?" he gleans. "You shouldn't have." His gentle teasing leaves me feeling on edge when I catch the slight undertone of menace behind it. I watch as he inspects his merchandise.

He's a beautiful man. Fair of skin and hair, prominent cheekbones, and pale blue eyes laced with bits of silver. He is tall and lean, with hardly a trace of fat on his body—not that I had the opportunity to prove that theory. Mr. Vrana was most definitely the type of man you would mix business and pleasure with, if not for your basic instincts yelling at you to run away screaming. He slants a smile my way. One

19

that sends a bout of shivers up my spine.

"I hope everything is to your liking?" I nibble at the sandwich on my plate. The beef is deliciously tender and juicy, set off only more by the slight smear of horseradish between it and the bread.

He pulls the black box from the bag and lifts its lid carefully, eyes alight with a victorious gleam. The crystal he pulls from its cushioned bed is a mixture of purple and pink. The cluster of three is just one part of something bigger, or so one jagged side seems to suggest.

"That's all he had on him," I inform Mr. Vrana carefully.

"I'm well aware," he replies shortly. We sit in silence as he repackages his new purchase. "This will go beautifully in my safe," he informs me genially. My smile begins to ache as it ticks up another inch.

"Wonderful."

He passes a cool eye over me. "You've done well. As per usual, Ms. Montgomery."

Well, *duh*. I was made for this kind of stuff. No one ever expected the pretty blonde laughing away in a crowd to have their most coveted belongings tucked safely away in the Hermes bag on her arm.

"Thank you, Mr. Vrana. It's always a pleasure doing business with you." A smile curves onto his lips, though it does not reach his eyes. It rarely does.

"You'll find your payment in progress, Ms. Montgomery. Should there be any issues, which I'm sure there won't, you know who to contact."

"Of course," I reply smoothly, fingers itching to

snatch my champagne as he stares me down. Mr. Vrana is a dangerous man, more so than any I have met before, and he knows it.

"I'll be debuting a new artist in the city next Saturday at my residence atop the Four Seasons," he tells me casually. I cannot hide the flicker of confusion that passes over my face. Nor the tiniest quiver in my smile at this unusual small talk. "I know your love of art," he continues, smile turning sharp, "and thought to extend to you an invitation. As long as you can keep your hands to yourself, that is."

"I—" *don't make a fool of yourself, Quinn, not now* "—would love to come. Thank you for the invitation." He inclines his head towards me and stands. This time I stand as well and stretch out my hand for him to take. He does, and places a kiss onto my knuckles, eyes never straying from my face. There is something unnerving about the act. The cool touch of his skin against my own. The uncommon pull of his gaze. It elicits a shiver from my body.

"Expect a formal invitation at your hotel's reception desk. The Omni, is it?" I nod numbly, counterfeit smile back in place. "Was the Warwick no longer to your tastes? Or Hotel Teatro?"

I quell the urge to shudder at his all-knowing smile. Of course, he's had me followed. It would hardly serve his purpose for me to turn tail and run off with his fancy rock.

"Something like that," I chime sweetly. He inclines his head then departs. Prada bag firmly in his grasp. I sit with a sigh, pick up my glass, and down its

21

contents. "*Damn*."

Popping a petit four into my mouth, I lean back and let my shoulders sag. I peruse the crowd once again, collecting my calm in bits and pieces. Another job was done. Another cool mill' in the bank. A few more jobs like this and I could retire before the end of next year. Vanish to some island and live out my days on some sandy beach sipping Mai Tais all day and night. Just me, myself, and I. And maybe a cabana boy or two to keep me company.

Something catches my eye. A familiar gleam of deep, cherry red hair. Elegantly curled and precisely draped. It's M. My mentor of sorts. Though she would loathe for me to call her so. Anything but M is simply unacceptable and yet I can't evade the word when she comes to mind. After all, M is the one who taught me the art of the con. How to seduce, how to steal, how to...*everything*. When I first started out selling forgeries, I was with some sleazebag who took advantage of my talents—among other things. It wasn't until M came along and convinced me of my worth and potential that I came fully under her tutelage.

She's on the arm of some older gentlemen dressed head to toe in Armani as they make their way out of the Tea Room. The maître d' passes them their umbrellas and raincoats. As if sensing my gaze, her own seeks mine. Our eyes meet, but no tell of recognition crosses her features. Then, after a long second passes by, I am gifted with a slight inclination of her head before she departs.

My phone is in my hand before I can help myself.
Fingers flying over the keyboard to send a message to
the redhead a second later. I receive her reply just as
I'm finishing off my last tea sandwich and let a real
smile come to fruition. A drink to catch up with a
colleague was just what I needed to distract from the
looming ache in my chest.

+++

"You look as if you're doing well, Q." A silky voice
greets from behind. I'm only halfway out of my chair
at La Menagerie before she presses two quick kisses to
the sides of my face and sits opposite me.

"Same to you, M," I respond sincerely. M is
somewhere in her early forties. A complete and total
fox. Dark red hair, deep brown eyes, and curves that
demand you listen. I was lucky that our first
encounter had gone the way it did. Instead of pressing
charges against me once she realized the lesser known
Pissarro I had sold her wasn't one at all, she informed
me I was wasting my talents. If I could learn to use
my womanly wiles, I'd see my payout double. Triple
even. The rest, as they say, is history. Five years later
and I was swimming in work.

"What trouble have you been getting into?" She
asks, her tone hinting at a secret. I cock my head.

"Nothing out of the ordinary," I reply. Her eyes
narrow on me as a glass of Pinot Grigio is poured for
each of us. She refrains from speaking until our waiter
is gone, our order in hand.

23

"Then why have I heard mention of your name through certain...channels?"

I give her a cheeky grin. "Hmm, perhaps they're just admirers of my work?" I suggest coyly, though inside her words strike a cord. "What were they asking for exactly?"

"Your name," she tells me after taking a deliberate sip of her wine. "Among other things."

My smile fades. "What 'other things'?" I ask tightly.

M smirks. "You're not going to make it very far in this business if you don't reign in that wild side of yours. I heard what happened in Montenegro."

"That was a complete misunderstanding," I assure her, smothering a smile as I recall the unplanned ménage à trois. "Which ended rather well, I might add. Everything went according to plan."

Her disapproval scolds me through her eyes. "You're too reckless, Q. Have you remembered anything I've taught you? You need to do your homework before accepting a job. Let alone jumping into a game on the side. You'll end up behind bars or six feet under if you don't start playing smarter." A plaintive sigh bursts past my lips, earning a rather feral glare from M. "I'm well aware of the excitement of it all. The rush of adrenaline while on the run. The surge of fear when rolling the dice. You can have that for as long as you want—"

"—As long as I play it smart," I finish.

"Let others lose themselves in you. Not the other way around."

I straighten in my seat. "I wasn't about to fall for the duke or his wife," I assure M.

She snorts, the action startling me. I had never heard her snort. Laugh. Giggle. Simper. Yes to all three. But never a *snort*. "As I said, you're too reckless. One of these times you're going to dive too deep. Hell, you'll probably even lose your heart to—"

"I wouldn't," I tell her sharply, feeling a frown starlight across my brow. I'd let my heart get trashed enough in the past by both family and friends. I had no desire to let the action happen again. So I had built a wall around my heart to put a stop to the endless stream of disappointments that passed through my life. I might be willing to risk life and limb, but no longer was my heart up for grabs. I was planning on keeping it to myself. Indefinitely.

Yet as the stubborn reassurance scores through my mind, flashes of dark hair and blue eyes stir from my memory. The taste of Kyle—the blistering heat of his hands and lips—assaults my senses like a phantom. A weak tremor falls from my nape to the end of my spine. A pang of longing not far behind.

M clears her throat and passes me a speculative look. "*Good.* And have you been covering your trail as I taught you to?" I flush and mentally tick off all the things I know I've yet to do.

"*Yes—*"

"—The one meant to keep you out of jail?" she asks calmly, her wine glass held lightly between her fingertips.

I give pause. Damn her. "I'll do better," I lament.

25

The waiter returns with our order of ahi tuna tartare before M can rip me a new one.

"No new clients are going to take you if you're so easily found, Q. Anonymity is important in this business of ours. For both you and the client."

I duck my head. "I understand, okay? I'll do better. This is all I have, and I don't particularly feel like screwing it up." She shrugs her shoulders and lets the subject drop, her admonishment over. I know she does it because somewhere in that deep dark heart she cares about me, but it's no less annoying to be treated like I'm still some novice. M homes in on the tartare. Taking a large helping of the tuna on one of the wonton chips. She lets out a hearty moan.

The sound, so similar to the one I'd made only a few days ago, submerges me in memories once more. Of Kyle's hungered kiss and how it felt to be devoured and savored all at once. The overwhelming sensation of a fire blazing through my veins as he held me prisoner. I squirm in my seat and reach for the tuna, shoving a loaded wonton into my mouth. M's barely disguised disgust brings my head back up from deep waters.

"So, who was the man you were with earlier?" I ask.

"Another long con job," she replies. "I saw that you were with Mr. Vrana. I've worked with him on a job or two before."

"He's intense. Don't you think?"

"To say the very least," she confirms, an uneasy look filtering across her face. "Be careful with him, Q.

He's not a man to be trifled with."

"Nobody we work with is meant to be trifled with."

Her sharp glare freezes me mid-reach. "I mean it, Q."

"He likes my work, and he pays well. *Really well,* M. I'm not about to mess that up."

"Just be smart. Especially with him. Are you staying in Denver much longer? Or are you working another job for him?"

I mull over the question as I chew on another hearty bite of the tartare. A dozen different coastal towns and beaches flitter across my mind's eyes. It had been a while since I'd indulged in a vacation of sorts where I could let loose and enjoy myself. Nevertheless, I still needed to stockpile my savings. Especially after my most recent shopping spree. I take a sip of my wine, eyeing M over the rim of the glass casually. She might be my mentor, but it wouldn't be the first time she learned of a job I was up for and swiped it from me.

"Just one more I think. I haven't received any of the recon for it yet."

"Well, I think you should get out of town." I arch a brow in response.

"I was just out of town," I remind her.

"Ah yes, traipsing around in paradise. How taxing."

I smirk, "It was an easy enough job." And easy enough to remember. In *vivid* detail. There was no denying it. I couldn't seem to keep my head out of the clouds. Every wandering thought led to blue eyes and charming grins that had felt so right when dealt my way. "A classic set up," I continue, forcefully nonchalant.

"Men are so predictable," she says with a languid sigh, not noticing my melancholy. "Isn't that nice? It always makes the job a little bit smoother. Was the target anyone of consequence?"

"Maybe," I reply, collecting myself. *Finally.* "I was given a time and place. A description of the object, and a photograph of the target. Nothing more."

M takes the last bite of the tartare and wipes away any lingering crumbs from her fingertips with the black napkin on her lap.

"A clean cut job then?"

"Very much so," I confirm. Except for the fact that I couldn't get Kyle out of my head. M shoots me a coy look over the rim of her wine glass.

"I have a little present for you."

"Is it Gucci?" She laughs and slips me a manila envelope from her purse. "Definitely, not Gucci," I gripe playfully.

"It's an opportunity," M informs me. She tinkers through her purse and pulls out a mirror and lip gloss.

"Who's paying?"

"No one," my eyes shoot to hers. "Like I said, it's an opportunity. A little birdie told me a Degas was making its way to some town called Branson Falls, up in Montana."

"You're joking."

I hold my breath as she gives me a candid smile. The one that softens her features and brings a real

light of joy to her eyes. "Really. Go ahead and look."
She busies herself with retouching her makeup as I
open the job.

"How is this...I can't believe this is happening.
How did I not hear about this?" I mutter under my
breath as I finger through the files: purchase order,
authentication papers, shipping details, schematics of
the house. "Who the hell is your little birdie friend,
and can I be friends with them too?" I give her my best
puppy dog eyes.

She laughs once more. "We all have our sources,
dear. Even you. Consider this an early birthday gift."

"You don't know when my birthday is," I remind
her, tucking the manila envelope into my purse. "*I*
don't even know when my birthday is."

"That's more useful than you realize, darling," she
purrs, finishing the reapplication of her lip gloss with
a flourish. A far away ache gives a knock to my heart.
Images of my mother, too doped up to care about her
only daughter's birthday year after year filtering
across my memory. I push the ache and memories
away back into the recesses of my heart.

"I'll be sure to take full advantage of it in a few
years."

She hums her agreement and begins to stand,
laying two crisp twenty-dollar bills on the table. "Take
advantage of this opportunity, Q. It's right up your
alley."

I blow her a kiss goodbye and watch as she fades
effortlessly out of view. Then I take out the manila
envelope once more and run through each document

another time, my heart racing all the while. This was the perfect birthday gift. The perfect project to keep my mind occupied.

I'd have to send a thank you card to this Mr. Adolphus once his Degas was safely in my possession.

Happy birthday to me.

CHAPTER 3
- Ryatt -

She arrived on Tuesday to scope out the town, choosing to shack up in the Cremosi's Bed and Breakfast. A quaint Colonial-style home with only one other occupant: Keenan. I had tasked him with trailing her whereabouts due to his military background, while I lurked from other, darker corners to mollify the soulmark. It had been a long four days. Having no contact, physical or otherwise, had left me in quite the state. My usual delightful personality and perfectly timed quips had been replaced quickly with a surly scowl and sarcastic remarks. Thankfully, both smile and scowl looked equally handsome on my face (to no one's surprise).

She had scouted our property for some time the following day, obviously readying herself for the delivery scheduled for Thursday. Watching her covert vigil from so near brought me nearly to madness. Her scent rode on the ends of each passing breeze,

taunting me from my place in the shadows. The
soulmark and beast inside howled at me to take her.
To mark and bind her to me before she had another
chance to leave me. Lucky for her, my patience and
foresight held. Even through my darkest of cravings.

Now all there was to do was wait just a bit longer.

The digital clock read 1:52 a.m. in blaring red. It
was exceptionally annoying, but the clock was
strategically placed. Just like every other object in the
room. I had made sure every piece and player had
adhered to my plan this afternoon and evening. The
delivery arrived on time, with Xander handling the
reception and having the piece brought up to the west
wing. It was placed in a room undergoing renovations,
or so it would seem to anyone looking in from afar. Old
canvas blankets, dirtied with dust and paint, were laid
across the room's furniture. Plastic lining was draped
carefully along each wall, and buckets of paint were
left surreptitiously about the room. The Degas was
placed carefully atop one of the side tables, left
uncovered and leaning lightly against the wall near
the insufferable clock. Both were placed directly across
from a window left slightly ajar. As if to suggest the
room needed airing.

What better temptation could I provide?

I sit amid the array, just out of sight and hidden
among the larger furniture to wait out my little thief.
My hands do not shake as they press the crystal full of
Woodford Reserve to my lips. I inhale purposefully,
filling my nose with the aroma of leather and honey.
Trace notes of butterscotch and toasted oak. It does

not burn as it slips past my tongue and down my throat. It engulfs my senses. Provides the distraction I need.

The clock lets out an inaudible click as the number two changes to three. I smile and sink lower into my seat. *Soon.*

+++

Quinn

Everything was going well. *Really well.* I arrived on Tuesday late in the afternoon after grabbing some supplies from a buddy of mine. The town was...cute. Quaint, even. Totally not to my tastes, but, whatever. It had a certain *je ne sais quoi* about it that somehow eased the ache in my heart. Or maybe it was just the thrill of doing a heist for myself that lifted my spirits.

At least the town had some taste. Boutiques with stylish clothes dotted the downtown area with price tags that would give a fair few pause. Bistros and cafés were filled with people. Their clever little chalkboard signs drawing in crowds.

"*Rise and Grind,*" outside of Luna Café.

"*Mojitos in Training,*" a staked sign within a small planter of mint near the entryway of Coco's.

"*We love our coffee like Kanye loves Kanye,*" at some hole-in-the-wall barista joint.

I survey the neighborhood and house I'll be pilfering. The subdivision screams money with its sprawling yards that bump up against the forest

33

preserve just beyond its white picket fences. The house I study is perhaps the biggest of them all. It looks like some old French estate set up against a backdrop of lush green trees and hills. I adore it. I'm sure inside there is a treasure trove of lavish trinkets and antiques. Ones that would fetch a tidy sum, but it's not what I came for. This afternoon the Degas was delivered. Mr. Adolphus collected the painting and ushered the delivery men inside, and to my delight, into the most easily accessible room. Despite it being on the second floor, the room offered two windows, one of which framed the Degas perfectly, even from afar.

It's nearing two o'clock in the morning. The house has been still for hours, and my back has long since started to ache from my position in the tree I occupy. I eye the garden trellis secured against the side of the house and the flowers that creep up along the lattice work. Climbing the trellis wouldn't be difficult knowing that I wouldn't have to keep my balance attempting to open one of the windows. Thank goodness they were remodeling the room and had left one of the windows cracked.

It was now or never.

I've packed light. A small knife, my lock pick kit, and art tube are all that I carry. I wear all black, *obviously*, and even a dark cap over my tightly braided hair. I land with a light grunt and take off across the great lawn in a low sprint, not anticipating lights to blare so suddenly from the back porch. I dive off into the shadows, heartbeat in my throat as I scamper to the side of the house. The lights click off a minute later, and still I wait, breathing in short, panicked gasps.

Nobody had seen me approaching. I was sure. They were just those lights programmed to turn on at any odd movement. With my luck, if anyone had peeked out a window, they would have assumed it to be some woodland creature. Like a bunny or a deer. Or some other woodland creature.

Once I've got my heart rate under control, I tiptoe along the side of the house, positioning myself under the open window. Then up I go. Past the trenches of violets and fuchsias until I reach the window sill. The window, already cracked open, slides up the rest of the way easily enough. It gives no wary cry of disbelief as I slip myself inside.

Adrenaline courses through my veins. Any traces of nervousness departing as I creep towards the Degas. A small shiver runs its way down from the base of my neck. It is stunning. Every portrait he has ever painted is alive with fluidity and movement that dance right off the canvas. It will be the centerpiece of my small collection. I release a slow, steady stream of air and inch forward. My palms feel sweaty in their leather casing, but that is a trivial matter. I only need to undo the framing and remove the canvas. All done quickly enough with items in my lock-picking arsenal.

"Hello, *Mary*." My stomach drops at the familiar voice, hands freezing in place as they reach for my prize. *Fuck.* "Tell me something, was it my bubbly personality or the thought of getting me back in your bed that brought you back to me."

Just take a deep breath, Quinn, I tell myself.
Steady that stupid heart of yours and play along 'til
you can make your getaway. Degas or not. Probably
not. I cast a look of longing towards the immaculate
portrait, a groan of disappointment growing in my
throat before I thrust it away. I take one step back
and turn to face Kyle.

"Couldn't get enough of me, could you?" His eyes
gleam even in the darkness, the moon, almost at its
full, shining down through the window onto him. How
the fuck didn't I see him? I put on my brightest smile,
eyes sharp as they adjust to the lighting or lack
thereof. His midnight hair gleams in the moonlight, a
tragic smirk upon his face that twists my stomach into
knots.

"I wasn't expecting to see you here," I answer
carefully.

"Ah, but I was expecting you, Mary." The ice cubes
in his glass rattle as he finishes off his drink. "I'm
sorry," he carries on unperturbed, "Would you prefer I
call you Quinn?"

My blood runs cold and my back stiffens. A
thousand thoughts run through my head until they
settle on one nugget of information. "I suppose I can
safely assume it was you who was digging into my
past?" My upper lip curls into a sneer. Damn it all to
hell; this was a setup. Some kind of payback for
stealing the crystal. *Or maybe he just wanted to see
me again.* The thought skirts quickly through my
mind, bringing an unusual wave of hope with it. I
squash it down like a bug.

"Guilty as charged."

"Gee, I don't know whether to be flattered or disgusted by your stalkerish tendencies," I tell him sweetly. His smile kicks up another notch, and he leans forward until his elbows rest upon his knees.

"You're trouble, Ms. Montgomery. I have a feeling we're going to get along famously."

I scoff, "We're not going to be doing anything together, anytime soon." I shuffle back a step, but still when his eyes narrow.

"You took something that belonged to me. It was very important. I'm going to need it back."

"I don't exactly have it on me," I snap, "Besides, finders keepers and all that."

He matches my wry smirk with one of his own, the chair he sits in letting out a whine as he shifts his weight. I swallow discreetly.

"What an interesting code you keep. Any others I should be made aware of?"

I mull over his question for a moment. "Never leave your drink unattended in a bar?"

His smirk tightens just barely around the edges. "Funny too—be still my heart. Why don't you take a seat, Quinn, so that we can have a little chat?"

My feet stay firmly planted beneath me as our gazes wage war. He leans back. I cock a hip and cross my arms.

"I'm afraid I can't stay and chat," I finally reply, batting my eyelashes.

"I'm sorry," he says with a good-natured laugh, "let me rephrase. Sit here," his finger stabs at the footstool next to his chair, "and have a bit of a chat with me. If all goes well, I see no reason why you can't leave unscratched."

My eyes steal towards the window, but Kyle makes a disapproving noise from his seat. Swallowing, I steel my nerves and look back towards him. A dark promise hovers at the edge of his expression.

"*Sit.*"

I hold back my huff of indignation and, head held high, stride towards the footstool, dusting off its surface before I sit upon it.

"Isn't this nice," he drawls, "a little midnight rendezvous to spice up a rather dull Thursday evening."

"It's Friday," I correct. "Technically."

"Technically." He agrees.

The room fills itself with the most awkward silence imaginable. His eyes drilling into the side of my face as I look anywhere but him. M was going to kill me; that is, if I didn't kill her first. Had she known about the setup? Had she been a part of Kyle's plan? I cast him a sidelong glance and catch his eye. A rush of blood floods my cheeks, but I turn it to my advantage.

"Did she say why she did it?" I ask, letting a quiver of uncertainty hedge my words. Kyle's brows pull towards each other in confusion.

"Who?"

I swallow and duck my head, hear the hammer of my heart beat out in my ears. "Stephanie." My eyes dart to him as I speak the false name, hope and distress dashed across my face.

38

He raises a brow quizzically before leaning towards me. "I can assure you that the path that led you here was made entirely by me. Your little Stephanie was merely a pawn moved so that the lure made it in front of you." I can't help the way my shoulders sag in relief. She didn't sell me out, but I had still been played. I straighten and cut Kyle a grim smile.

"I hope you're not waiting for congratulations."

Kyle grins once more. "I would never be so presumptuous, but one can hope."

Before I have a chance to protest he snatches the hand I have curled anxiously around the edge of the footstool. He brings it to his lips in a chaste kiss, eyes never leaving mine. A flutter erupts in my stomach. Some strange kindling of feeling stealing over my nerves. His touch inspires thoughts of him and I together, laughing over inside jokes and stealing kisses in darkened corners. But most of all it triggers an almost immediate heat to tumble through me. I press my thighs together sharply with a gasp and attempt to yank back my hand, but to no avail. I glower at him in response.

"No touching, *Kyle*," I spit, yanking once more. He releases me unexpectedly, and I careen backward, footstool and all. My screech cuts short when the stool beneath me is caught, and a hand placed possessively on my waist. Kyle's face is suddenly inches from my own.

"It's Ryatt," he breathes, all traces of jest gone from his voice.

39

"Excuse me?" comes my somewhat breathless response, eyes comically wide at our nearness. My seat is gently righted, and Ryatt kneels before me on one knee, maintaining his close proximity.

"My name is Ryatt. Your name," he says softly, "is Quinn 'no middle name' Montgomery."

There is something about this claustrophobic space that numbs my mind and stalls my heart. The warmth of his hand creeps past the layer of my black leggings and soaks into my skin. Unable to help myself, my eyes flutter nervously as they lock on his lips. In the next instant they lock back upon his eyes. *Don't go there, Quinn.*

He must see the uncertainty behind them as I try to take control of my frenzied nerves. There is something about the way his smile softens. A touch of vulnerability slipping through it like an offering. He does not move closer, but he does sink lower onto his heel.

"Why did you come looking for me?"

His gaze tightens, his eyes sinking deeply into my own to hold me hostage. "I've told you," he says slowly, "you took something from me. I need it back, Quinn." I shift uneasily in my seat.

"I told you. I don't have it."

Ryatt: such a fitting name for this bundle of mayhem. He doesn't look pleased with my answer. Not one bit. And yet...and yet, he does not sharpen his gaze upon me as others might have. Yell and bash at me with words or fists. He simply bows his head in thought for a moment, grip tightening on my waistline just a fraction.

"Well now, that's a problem, sweetheart. I'll be needing you to get that back for me."

My eyes widen in alarm. "What?"

He tilts his face back up. Licks his lips and smiles. "I'll need you to fetch the crystal back for me."

My cheeks flame, "One, I'm not some dog. I don't fetch. And two, I can't."

"Can't or won't?"

"Both," I snarl. "It's impossible. I can't just go back and steal from the guy that paid me to steal it from you. That's just...wrong." He gives me an incredulous look.

"You steal things for a living. What does it matter if you steal something back for a better payout? I'll double his price," Ryatt reasons.

M's words echo in my head. How I shouldn't be tempted to cross a man like Mr. Vrana. How there would be consequences. I was already halfway through his second job proposal, having gotten it with the invitation for his gallery opening. My head shakes firmly side-to-side.

"I'll be labeled a double-crosser. I can't. I'm—" I grimace "—sorry."

"I'm afraid sorry isn't good enough. My brother and our pack are counting on me to deliver. Not only them, but our allies as well."

I frown. "Your pack? You mean your gang?"

Ryatt's hand slips from my waist to the back of his neck as he lets out a heavy sigh. "Not gang. Pack, but I can explain."

"Don't," comes my rushed reply. "Let's just put all this behind us and move forward." A sour expression crosses his features: lips thinning, cheeks hollowing, brow going cross.

"I'm afraid I can't quite let this one go."

"Well, I'm afraid you have no say in the matter. I'm not stealing back the crystal. End of story." I move to stand, but he is quick to tug me back into my seat. His hand a sudden vice around my wrist.

"What was it you said earlier?" he inquires smoothly. "Finders keepers?" His grip tightens to emphasize his point.

My breathing comes in shallow pants. "You can't 'finders keepers' people, you creep," I hiss, though a thrill of unexpected excitement races up my spine.

"Ah, I dare to disagree Ms. Mont—oomph!" I thrust myself upward, knee driving into Ryatt's chin with my momentum. He topples down, arms flailing to catch his fall and check his injury simultaneously. I dash towards the window; the Degas left sadly behind.

I barely make it down the garden trellis fast enough. It shakes unsteadily with my jerky movements, and by the time I've made it down Ryatt is leaning halfway out the window, a smear of red down his chin.

"There's no use in running, Quinn," he calls down as I take hasty steps back. "I've men out front waiting to retrieve you, and you wouldn't make it out in the—"

I don't bother to wait for his unnecessary warning. If there were men in the front, my only chance was the forest. I would just have to loop around and make it back to my car a few blocks away. There's no time to turn back to see if he follows. I must focus all my attention on escaping and outrunning him. My lungs are burning by the time I reach the edge of the forest, and only then do I dare chance a glance over my shoulder. A cry of disbelief catches halfway past my lips. He has nearly halved the distance between us.

I feel a sudden panic flood my system. It pushes me faster, until I feel the pounding of my heart streaming through my outstretched legs and pumping arms. A violent shudder rages past my lips as I hear his excited breath near. Before I can blink, before I can process just how the fuck this all went wrong, I am hurtling towards the ground, a steely arm wrapped tightly around my middle.

We tumble into the ground, skidding to a painful halt.

"Get off me!" I shriek, pushing and struggling against him. He grunts with the effort to keep me still, working my hands above my head and trapping my legs down with his knees. "Get off!" I cry, trembling from both fear and pain. I can feel the warm flow of blood at the back of my head and feel my energy depleting fast.

"Just calm down. I'm not going to hurt you."

"Like hell, you aren't!" I screech.

"Calm down," he snarls down at me, shoving his face right into mine. I gasp in horror as I watch his eyes dilate and bleed gold.

"What the fuck?" I gasp. Tears blur my vision, but not enough to hide what I have seen. "What the fuck!"

43

Ryatt stares at me in a panic, his eyes rapidly dissolving into blue, then back to gold again as he quakes above me.

"Just...calm down," he pleads. Except I can't. There is blood rushing to my head too quickly, and spilling out the back of it much too fast. Black spots appear briefly and then I drift into darkness.

CHAPTER 4

- Quinn -

I am incensed.

Practically foaming at the mouth, having awoken
to find myself in a prison cell. Except this wasn't your
ordinary prison cell. The bars were thicker and
cleaner looking than any dingy cell you might actually
find in a prison or police station. No. This was some
high-grade shit. The door to my cage had no lock and
key mechanism but instead relied on some magnetic
or electronic signature to open it. Not that it would
matter if it were the former instead of the latter. My
lock pick kit had been taken, along with anything else
that might have aided me.

I desperately wanted to hit something but didn't
particularly feel like splitting my knuckles in the
process. *Ugh.* How I had slept through the night was a
mystery to me. Did that normally happen when a
person fainted? I had never fainted before.

I had also never been caught before, minus that

first time with M.

"Fuck. Me." I groan, resting my head against the cold metal bars.

I shoot a nasty glare at the camera and its annoying red light, set high in the corner across from my cell. My middle finger raises in salute before I turn away from it with a scoff. Not only had I been played, but I had been caught. I wasn't sure which was more bruised: my head or my ego. I tried to comfort myself with the fact that they couldn't keep me down here forever. Wherever "here" was. Probably a closed-off portion of the basement meant for gang business or some weird, dirty sex exploits. If I were lucky, it would be the gang business.

A noise sounds from afar. The weighty impression of a door closing, perhaps? I stir backward towards the cot I woke up on, and sit. I squeeze my eyes shut and try to block out the hammering of my heart to listen for the sound of footfalls. After a minute of nothing, I flop backward in defeat.

"Damn," I whisper to nobody.

And then the door at the far end of the room slams open.

"Good morning, Quinn!" Ryatt announces. I jolt upwards. He looks obnoxiously happy. Fresh clothes and a bright smile on his face. He holds a tray in his hand filled with food and drinks. My heart and stomach lurch at the pleasant sight. "I come bearing gifts." Gifts indeed. No doubt he meant to lure me into some sense of security with his peace offering. I needed to play this smart, which meant I needed to bring out *Jessie "Smooth as Ice" Williams*. Playing her part had gotten me out of a number of scrapes.

"Is one of them the key to this cell?"

"It could be," he says, coming to stand in front of the cell. "If you play your cards right. Breakfast?"

"What time is it?" The words come out with more bite than I intend as I watch him set the tray down on some small metal table against the wall. I rake my eyes over him. His clothes look tailored and pressed. His face clean shaven. A familiar burst of heat spreads from my neck to my cheeks and chest.

"Just before seven, darling." I grit my teeth as he catches me staring, a knowing look in his eyes. "Tea?"

"I'm more of a coffee kind of girl."

He feigns a contrite look. "I'm afraid tea's all we've got at the moment. You'll have to make do." He takes the mug from the tray and walks up to the cell, holding it carefully outside the bars. *Jerk.*

I stand slowly, smoothing back the hair that has come loose from my braid. He looks so pleased with himself it makes me want to vomit. I reach the bars and wait expectantly for him to pass the mug. He raises an eyebrow and pulls it back ever so slightly. Men and their power plays.

"Are you going to give me the tea, or not?" I snap.

"You just have to reach out and take it yourself, darling." I do so with an annoyed huff, ignoring the shit-eating grin on his face.

"I'd prefer if you called me by my name. You know, the one you spent so much time looking for?" I blow at the steam rising from the mug, dipping a finger in

47

quickly to test the temperature. It was much too hot to drink.

"Oh, I didn't have to look very hard to find your name. Your history. Your life story, which I must say, was quite fascinating. Tell me, Quinn, shouldn't that information be a little bit harder to find in your line of business?"

Mother fucker.

"Are you calling me a bad name in your head?" he croons, taking a step forward and leaning casually against the cell bars. The shit-eating grin turns into a shit-eating smile. "Is it very *naughty?*"

I take a breath. Blow it out over the tea and take a scalding sip. "Is this some kind of weird sex dungeon?"

Ryatt bursts out in laughter, taking a long moment to find his composure before repositioning himself against the bars. He leans both hands above his head and the gray polo he wears rides up to show a glimpse of tanned, taut skin. "It could be," he purrs, noticing my wandering eyes.

"Is this how you usually sweep your conquests off their feet? Kidnapping?"

He runs his tongue along his teeth. The smile on his face positively indecent. "I assure you, I've never come to such drastic measures." He places a hand over his heart. "Scout's honor."

"Yet, here I am."

"Croissant?" He offers casually, sweeping out an arm back to the tray. "You must be starving." I take another drag from the mug.

"I'm more of a waffle girl," I tell him with a short

shrug. His eyes gleam at the information, but he fetches the croissant regardless. I stave off the frown that begs to fall on my brow. Why I decided to share that personal piece of information was beyond me. Maybe I was concussed? I had to be if I found myself being somewhat reluctantly impressed with Ryatt's rather successful scheme to get me here.

"Myself, as well," he confesses, passing me the croissant through the bars. The buttery pastry is warm in my hand. I take a tentative bite. "Good?"

I nod and lick the flakes of pastry off my lips. Keep my eyes at half-mast as I watch him, watching me. "Yes," I tell him softly, and wash down my bite with the tea. M was right; men were so easy. So predictable.

His eyes narrow. For a moment, I dare think I see some semblance of gold hint around the irises. My heart gives a little shudder as memories from last night crop up. I try to busy my mind with the food and drink I've been gifted, but the more I try, the more I see blazing gold eyes and the flash of sharpened canines. What exactly had I seen last night? I pass a coy look to Ryatt as I finish off the croissant. There was no need to alert him of my growing uncertainty.

"I'm not going to hurt you," he murmurs, "though I have a right mind to punish you in some manner after everything that's happened this past week. Drugging me. Stealing from me. Running from me when I explicitly asked you not to." He ticks my grievances off on his fingers, eyes alight with something close to delight as he watches for my reaction. "Tell me, are

49

you fond of spanking? When done right it can be both
a punishment and a reward."

I almost spit out my tea at his innocent tone.
Instead, the tea makes itself halfway down my throat
and up my nose. He laughs outright at my coughing
fit. A fact I will not easily forget. It takes a minute for
the coughing to subside, but the uncomfortable
tightening in my throat and wetness up my nose will
take longer.

"Seriously?" I bite out.

He places a hand over his heart. Rolls his
shoulders back to stand just that bit straighter. "Of
course, darling. Tell me. Spanking: yes or no?"

The glare I bestow would melt glaciers. Start
forest fires. I rise from the bed and take a menacing
step forward, lips pulling back in a snarl to reply.
"*Yes.*"

Ryatt rewards me with a gigantic smile. I gasp in
horror and place a hand across my traitorous lips.

"I mean—yes!" I shout, followed by a short shriek.
My hand goes back over my mouth. What the hell was
going on? The persona of Jessie quickly drops, leaving
just plain old Quinn in her wake. God help me.

"Excellent." His smile digs deeply into his cheeks
to stop from laughing outright once more. Bastard.

"I didn'—" I cringe as my throat contracts, and my
tongue becomes laden. "I didn'—*ugh*! Why can't I talk?
Why can't I say what I want to say?"

"Remember, Quinn. Honesty is always the best
policy."

"What the fuck is that supposed to mean?" I try to

rein in my temper, I really do, but I can actually feel the heat radiating off my cheeks and neck. It certainly doesn't help that he looks so damn pleased with himself. He bites his tongue, blue eyes sparkling mischievously before darting to the floor then back at me.

"It means you shouldn't lie. Or attempt to for that matter." I take a steadying breath and squeeze the mug in my grasp. I shouldn't attempt to lie, what could that possibly—*oh*. My eyes focus on my half-finished tea. Whatever it had been laced with was obviously fast working.

"You drugged me?" I ask incredulously. So much for reining in my temper.

"Fair's fair, darling. A little *lunaria* tea to keep you honest." I hurtle the mug across the cell, but Ryatt is quick enough to move out of the splash-and-crash radius. He eyes the mess I've made with a wry grin before returning to his spot.

"You are unbelievable," I seethe.

"That's what most women say after we've—"

"Don't!" I shout. "Do not finish that sentence."

Ryatt licks his lips but nods in agreement. "Right then, on to more mannered subjects. About last night..."

"You mean the part where you chased me down and then kidnapped me?"

"No, neither of those."

"You mean the part where your eyes went all glowy, and your teeth got all pointy?" The question tumbles from my lips before I can stop them, and we

51

both freeze. *Fuck.* I did not mean to say that. How long was this drug going to be in my system? This honesty crap was getting old, fast.

"You remember that, do you?" he asks soberly. The cool undertones of a threat permeate his voice. "Anything else?"

I take a moment to ponder my word choice, smiling sweetly once I finally answer. "Those are the most prevalent." His jaw ticks as he puts on a strained smile.

"Where is the crystal, Quinn?"

"Not on me," I retort, crossing my arms over my chest as I cock a hip to the side.

"If it's not on you," he responds, "then where is it?"

My throat contracts, the truthful answer pushing up and past my lips uncomfortably. "With my boss."

"And who would that be?"

My chest pulses with anxiety. "A man." Ryatt huffs.

"A man whose name is..."

I do my best to hold back the words, to fight the discomfort that slowly turns into pain. Yet the pressure that builds stunts my breathing, and so, in a rasping gasp I respond, "Mr. Vrana." My eyes shut in defeat and I allow my arms to pull around my chest a bit more tightly.

"Mr. Vrana?" Ryatt seems to be speaking more to himself than me, so I turn my back to him and take several deep breaths. I had just signed away my life. If Ryatt didn't finish me off down here, then Mr. Vrana most certainly would. He would find me, torture me,

and—"You're certain it was a Mr. Vrana who solicited
your services? Tall, Slavic features, a bit on the pale
side?"

I clench my teeth and nod my head. "Yes," I hiss,
turning back around to face him. Ryatt takes a step
back and begins to pace; a studious frown planted
firmly on his face.

"Do you know what that crystal is?"

I shrug, "I don't know. Just another priceless
crystal to add to someone's collection." Ryatt stops and
fixes me with a scowl.

"You've gone and got yourself mixed up in
something far greater than you could have imagined,
little girl."

"I'd hardly call myself a little girl. Or is that just
the type you like sucking you off?" Ryatt snarls at me,
that same flash of gold striking like lightning across
his eyes. "*What are you?*"

He quells his temper quickly, cutting off his sound
of displeasure and replacing it with a magnificent
glare. "Behave, Quinn. Or you won't be leaving this
cell anytime soon." I hold back my retort, waiting for
the pounding of my heart to simmer. Though his
unworldly anger was evident, I wasn't frightened. Not
exactly, anyway. Ryatt was a different kind of danger.
Volatile when provoked, but also a man who took
great measure in calculating each move he made. My
pulse thrummed oddly with anticipation at the game I
had fallen into.

"What are you?" I ask again.

"A lycan."

His answer gives me pause. I shuffle my weight from one foot to the other. "You mean, like, a *werewolf*?"

"Not even close, darling," he purrs, leaning up against the bars. A dark look clouds his face. "You think of a *werewolf*," he spits the word out with disdain, "and you image some terrifying creature, part-man part-beast, reared up upon hind legs to chase you through the woods at night. One bite, they tell you, is all it takes to share its fate. To transform into this monster every full moon. To lose control and find yourself reverted to your baser animal instincts." He gives pause to let his barbarous words sink in. "When I chase something or someone down...I'm very much conscious of my actions."

"You can't honestly expect me to believe this." A tingling sensation erupts across the back of my neck at his story. "Prove it," I demand before he can start up again. "If you're a werewolf, or a lycan, or whatever you want to call yourself, do it. Change. Right now." I issue the challenge in a strong voice, pushing past my trepidation.

Ryatt scowls. "I can't," he bites out roughly.

"Well, if you can't show me—"

"Surely I've already shown you enough," he says. "You said it yourself. My eyes and my teeth changed before your very eyes last night. Didn't they?"

The strange pull to tell the truth persists, but not nearly as strongly as five minutes ago. I keep my lips sealed, despite the discomfort.

"Lycans, dearest Quinn, are born. We are the

children of the moon, blessed to share our nature with that of the wolf who resides inside us. There was a time when we could transform freely into our wolf forms. When we could run together whenever we wished, be it on two feet or four, and then Merida came along. Merida was a very powerful witch several centuries ago. Scorned by the lycan she loved, she cursed the entirety of the lycan clan. Her intent was to bind our wolf halves so that they might never know freedom, but the power of the moon was too strong. As such, for centuries lycans have only been able to shift into our wolf forms when the moon is full, and we are at our most powerful."

"Right," I drawl. "So, you can only turn into a wolf on a full moon. Sounds a lot like a werewolf to me."

"There's a cure out there. A potion to release us from the curse."

"*Mmhm.*"

Ryatt's annoyance grows. "One day the cure will be found, and we will roam this earth as we were intended to—"

"—Like dogs," I chime sarcastically. Ryatt growls. Point to me.

"As wolves. As protectors of the night."

I scoff, "Protectors of the night? Against what? Vampires? Ghosts?" I let out an incredulous laugh.

"Against your Mr. Vrana," he tells me, voice going deadly calm.

The laugh dies in my throat. "Excuse me?"

"Has he ever touched you?"

"Excuse *you*," I all but snarl.

"He's quite cool to the touch, is he not?" My retort is ready on the tip of my tongue when I give his words the chance to sink in. My mind flicks back to our few brief face-to-face meetings. Aside from the odd handshake or kiss on the back of my hand, we did not touch. And yet he had been somewhat startlingly cold each time. Though it had seemed a bit warmer in recent encounters.

"What's your point?"

"My point is that generally speaking when one does not have a beating heart to circulate blood properly through the body, the body becomes cold."

"Some people just run cold," I tell him rationally.

"Or they're a vampire."

We stare each other down. "Listen, *Kyle*—"

"Ryatt," he snaps. Point to me. Again.

I smile demurely. "Right, *Ryatt*. I don't know who it is you're trying to convince here, but I'm not buying the whole supernatural werewolf theory."

"Lycan," he gripes, head falling forward to bang against the bars. "What about Mexico?" A flush skirts up my cheeks.

"What about it?"

"You can't tell me you didn't feel..." his head shoots upward, eyes wide as he stares at me with newfound chagrin. "Never mind," he mumbles, looking away and beginning his pacing once more.

"It was just a job," I remind him. "It wasn't anything more than that, alright?" A sting of displeasure wraps around my body as I force the words from my lips, caught in a half truth, half lie. We treat ourselves to another stilted silence, letting the tension grow thickly between us.

"Whether you believe me yet or not, the facts remain the same," he finally tells me. "You have now found yourself a key player in our supernatural game. You're going to work with us and get back the crystal, Quinn."

"I can't, Ryatt. I told you that already. A thousand times."

"You can, and you will."

I shake my head stubbornly. "I can't get it back. I don't know where it is. For all I know he's shipped it away to some hiding spot or he had it destroyed."

"He wouldn't destroy it," Ryatt comments, coming to a stop once more.

"You're right. It's not that pretty," I tell him with a half smirk. Ryatt returns it, eyes sparkling. A flash of something stirs in my stomach at our matching looks. I swallow and douse the feeling out.

"It isn't, but it's not an ornament to be placed in a house. It's a very powerful, magical artifact."

An exasperated sigh slips out. "Of course. How could I forget about the witches?"

"Be careful what you say, darling. My soon-to-be sister-in-law just so happens to be a witch."

"Oh really?" Not-werewolves and now witches? Did he seriously expect me to believe this crap?

"Really," he says with a smirk. "You can thank her personally for the tea."

"Maybe I will." *With my fist in her eye.*

"No need to look so cross. It seems the effects have

57

already worn off." He raises an eyebrow challengingly that I don't dignify with a response.

"If she's a witch, can't she just magic the crystal to herself or something? Why do I have to get it?"

"Certain properties of the crystal make it impossible to locate and summon. As to why you must be the one to get it, I thought that was obvious enough. You have a relationship with him. You have his trust."

"He will kill *me*," I tell him, voice cracking at the end. "I can't steal the crystal back, but I bet I could find you a new one—"

"That's not possible, I'm afraid," he tells me tightly after my soft declaration. "But I promise you, Quinn: he will not harm you." His impassioned words leave me slightly...breathless. Some stirring of feeling begins to grip my heart as I pull my refusal forward.

"I'm sorry," I reiterate. "I just can't."

Ryatt frowns. "Then I suppose it's time we spoke with my brother."

CHAPTER 5

- Ryatt -

She casts a wary glance my way as I open the cell door with a thumb drive, features rearranging into something more neutral as she catches my stare. I plaster a smile on my face and swing my body to the side, gesturing ahead of me. Quinn straightens her back and walks past me purposefully towards the door I entered through, her entire body coiled with tension. A nervous lamb waiting for its chance to escape the big bad wolf.

"I wouldn't try anything rash," I warn her. A slight stiffening runs along her spine and raises the hair on the back of her neck. I chase it all with my eyes and focus on every infinitesimal stretch and pull of her muscles. She's plotting her escape, no doubt. I can hear the race of her heart in tune with each calculated step she takes. Through the air wafts the smell of both adrenaline and small spikes of fear.

She would run. I would give chase. Again.

A grim smile slants across my face. "Take a left at the door. On your right you'll see a stairway. Go up."

Her steps speed up a fraction as she opens and slips past the basement door. Though I'm only a hairsbreadth behind, she still manages to the slam the door halfway closed on me. I catch it and slip around 'til I'm flush behind her suddenly frozen form.

"Meet Keenan," I whisper into her ear, eyeing the intimidating man. "Keenan, this is Quinn." He grunts in response, arms folded across his broad chest and an unpleasant scowl on his face. His arms are littered with tattoos, which bulge with muscles.

"I didn't realize you had reinforcements lurking about," she tells me, disdain evident. The bitter scent of fear spills into the hallway. Keenan and I share a look, then his arms drop to his side and his scowl retreats. Somewhat, at least. Resting bitch face is just as common in men as it is in women.

"Good morning," he rumbles. Then he tries for a smile. Quinn leans back slightly, breath held for one excruciating moment until it is released.

"Morning," she replies, all false-cheer.

"We're headed upstairs," I tell Keenan. He raises a brow, goes to cross his arms once more, then stops. A weird spasm of emotions flits across his face: frustration, annoyance, embarrassment, and finally, grim acceptance. It's always so amusing to watch him mind his manners. "To see Xander."

Keenan looks to me, then Quinn. "Good luck," he tells her, shooting a rather disarming grin her way as he relaxes. I send him a scowl over her shoulder, lightly pushing at her lower back to guide her forward and past Keenan.

"No need to be too friendly, brother" Keenan ducks his head sheepishly, though a sly smirk remains on his face.

"Good luck, *brother*," he replies under his breath so that only I might hear as we travel upwards. "You'll need it."

I huff, half exasperated, half amused, and slow my pace to put some distance between us. My eyes drift lower, eyeing the black material that fits faithfully along her legs and ass. The soulmark tingles as my cock stirs at the sight. Watching her ascent is certainly a pleasurable experience.

"Excuse you," she scolds, tossing a mean glare over her shoulder, though it doesn't quite meet her eyes. Her cheeks are fused with color, lips puckered into a delicious pout.

What a beauty.

"My apologies," I declare. The frown she wears deepens momentarily before she sets her sights back on the upcoming open archway. Her steps quicken once more. No doubt to get away from my scrutiny. *Or*...my head ticks to the side, ears perking to the sudden crescendo of her heart. "Quinn—"

She darts up the last couple of steps and throws herself down the hallway. Her footfalls sound swiftly against the carpet runner, but they are drowned out by my own. I catch her easily, my arm slipping around her middle to propel her against the wall. She hits the wall with a yelp, my arm acting as a slight cushion as

I push myself against her, trapping her body between my own and the wall.

"I thought I told you not to run," I tell her calmly, letting her soft panting sound against my collarbone. Her eyes do not look up to meet mine. Instead, they stare determinedly through me.

"You said not to do anything rash," she corrects.

"And running away isn't rash?"

She shrugs, wiggling against my hold. I stifle a groan. Her thigh is sandwiched tightly between my own. "It seemed the most sensible option in my current predicament." She peeks up at me. Pretty cerulean blue veiled against a stronghold of blonde lashes. *Minx.* She shifts her hips and places her hands tentatively against my chest. From runaway to coy damsel in under a minute. Impressive. Next she would be simpering out an apology before shoving against my chest to flee once more. I smile down at her.

I carefully peel off her hands and place them behind her into possession of one of mine. She glares up at me, fingernails biting into the flesh they can reach.

"Careful, Quinn. I'm beginning to think you want me to bend you over my knee right now." Color rises to her cheeks, and her eyes dart away. The familiar scent of her arousal fills the space between us. I press more firmly against her. My half hard-on swells to a full as I feel the warmth of her curves. "Or are you the type who prefers to be tied down as your punishment is doled out?"

I graze her cheekbone and across the way to her

bottom lip with my fingertips. She shivers at my touch, eyelashes fluttering closed as I duck my head down closer to her neck.

"No matter," I whisper on, the husky timbre of my voice slipping between us, "you'll be gagged." Her eyes startle open, staring at me in scandal as her breath continues in little puffs of hot air. The scent of her arousal nearly doubles, forcing me to bite back a moan. "We wouldn't want to disturb anyone with the noises you'd be making."

"You're vile," she tells me, fire in her voice and pounding through her veins.

I bury my nose in her neck and inhale deeply. I might be vile, but there's no denying her reaction to my indecent proposals. She smells heavily of arousal and adrenaline. I let my nose slip farther back along her neck and smile as I feel her skin break out in goosebumps.

The soulmark is so near; I could reach out my tongue and taste it. My hips give a small thrust forward, and I'm rewarded with one in kind. Her soft trembling moan fans my ear.

"We could be vile together," I say, nipping at her earlobe before pulling back. "If you'd like."

Her mouth opens and closes comically for a moment. Then a different flush rises to her cheeks. "Not likely," she growls.

I raise a skeptical brow, "There's nothing to say we can't mix business with pleasure." *And then more pleasure.* The wolf echoes its agreement in my head with a soft growl.

63

"I don't think so."

I hum knowingly, "And here I thought we had...chemistry."

She smirks cruelly back at me. "I'll take that as a compliment of doing my job well, but make no mistake, Ryatt, there is no chemistry between us." Her heart gives a little skip as she gives her rebuttal. *Liar.*

"Then would you care to explain your obvious excitement?"

"I'm not excited," she grinds out between her teeth, "just a decent actress."

Ah, but the nose knows, darling. "Remember, Quinn," I say lightly, "I'm of the lupine variety. Racing heart. Dilated eyes. That tempting moan and the smell of your arousal. They're all signs to the opposite."

"You're crazy." The scent of her embarrassment fills my nose. Time to turn it down a notch. No matter how hard it is to ignore the attraction between us. I can't recall Xander being so consumed by his soulmark so early on...I clearly hadn't given my Alpha enough credit.

"There's no need to be ashamed of your attraction," I tell her honestly and lick my lips a bit nervously. I remove all traces of humor from my voice. "I've certainly done a poor enough job of hiding my own. As it is," I venture softly, "I don't see why we might not take the chance to explore what could be between us after all this mess is sorted."

Time stands still, and then she guffaws. She stares pointedly at the spot just over my shoulder. A sharp dagger of dread penetrates my heart as I try to ignore the sting of her response.

"I don't think so," she says cruelly. "What exactly did you think was going to happen? You locked me up in some weird basement prison, and now you're trying to force me to steal back some *stupid* crystal. Not to mention the whole 'I'm a werewolf' angle you're trying to pull—which is really weird, by the way. You should just stick with the 'shallow playboy' routine you had down in Mexico. Seems truer to form, don't you think?"

Her aim is far too accurate. The words cut deep as intended, but I mask my pain with a menacing smile. "Let's not pretend like you have even an *inkling* of who I am, little lamb." She scowls at the endearment. "Other than the man who's able to bring you undeniable pleasure—"

"*Seriously?*" she gripes.

"You're right; how about a new topic? Rooming arrangements. This," I reach out a hand and knock on the doorframe a foot away, "is my room. You'll be staying in there with me. Ah, ah! No more talking, darling. You'll be made to stay downstairs in the cell if you can't manage to behave yourself. Besides, this way I can keep an eye on you. Make sure your wandering hands stay off all the precious cargo here. To be clear, I am speaking of myself."

"You're incorrigible." She tugs her arms from my grasp and pushes me away. While straightening her clothes she loses all scent of her earlier arousal, to be replaced with cool control.

"Among other things," I concur. "Shall we?" I point to a double door towards the end of the hall. She stalks past me without another word but stops just short of reaching them.

"Nice art collection," she murmurs, folding her arms over her chest as she waits for me to either reach her side or open the door.

"Thank you," I say somewhat stiffly, "it was my late mother's." Her eyes dart to my face, but I hold an unreadable expression.

"She had good taste. It's not exactly to my taste," she hedges somewhat kindly, "but beauty is in the eye of the beholder and all that crap."

"And your beauty is something akin to a Degas."

She smooths down her braided hair carefully. "Something like that."

+++

Quinn

I know my attention should be given fully to the situation at hand, but my mind keeps wandering back to the hallway. The way Ryatt had me pressed against the wall. His colorful descriptions of what he planned to do to me. The way my nipples had tightened almost painfully. How my panties still felt damp. Why did I feel such a strange pull towards him? It was as if my nervous system went up in smoke and flames every time he stepped too near. Maybe something more had been slipped into the tea than he let on? The attraction I felt wasn't ordinary.

The door opens to reveal a woman with golden brown skin, and hair swept back behind a large headband. She carries a tray with a teapot and teacup on it, hips swaying gently from side to side as she comes forward. I wrinkle my nose.

"I'm not thirsty," I tell them cheerfully, eyeing the singular teacup with distrust. "But thanks."

The newcomer sends me a pitying glance and then looks towards Xander, the "Alpha." He makes a study of me from behind his desk, eyes calculating my every movement. The weight of his regard is mildly stifling, a feat I had not thought possible after encountering Keenan.

"It's either the tea or the syringe," he tells me. My eyes dart over the tray once more and note the needle resting on a golden piece of cloth. I swallow.

"Tea."

The woman passes me another sympathetic glance to which I roll my eyes. If she wanted to help, she could. She chose not to. I wonder, is this "the witch" Ryatt was talking about?

"There's no need to be mad at her," Xander tells me calmly. "Your anger is more aptly served at us."

I scoff and take the proffered tea. "Please refrain from telling me who I should and should not be mad at. If I want to hate on the girl that's pouring me the spiked tea, then I will." I turn my steely gaze to the woman who stands serenely back. "*Thanks, sweetheart.*" She flinches as I slug back the scalding tea, tossing the teacup and saucer onto the desk with little regard.

"There's no need to be crude, darling," Ryatt cajoles from the chair next to mine.

"I'm not your fucking *darling*," I snap back. The room goes silent at my outburst, while I attempt to curb my baser emotions.

I take in a deep breath to calm my hammering heart. There wasn't anything I could do at the moment to get out of this. I just had to invest in the new game and let it play out. Maybe along the way, I could find a way to get the hell out, but for now, there would be no advantage to looking back. Once this was all over, I would take a new name, a new everything, and hope to God I would never be found again. After all, Ryatt said he would double my price, right? I take another deep breath.

"Well, safe to say we all know why you're here," Ryatt starts, voice perfectly nonchalant. Xander sends his brother a short, but stern glare.

"Ryatt," he says on an exhale, "it might be best if you didn't talk." Ryatt hardly looks offended, and upon catching my inspection he sends me a wink. *Honestly.* I roll my eyes toward the ceiling, dutifully ignoring the way I feel my cheeks fill with warmth at his flirtations.

"Of course, your wish is my command, brother."

Xander's eyes return to me. "Quinn, you stole a crystal from Ryatt a week ago."

"Six days ago."

Xander's furrowed brow does not break. "It was no ordinary crystal."

"So I've been told," I say with a smirk. "Something about witches and werewolves. If you ask me, it looks like one of those lamp things. You know, the ones that light up." My eyes shut as I try to recall the name of the object I'm imagining.

"A rock salt lamp?" Ryatt offers.

I snap my fingers and my eyes open. "Yes!" I send Ryatt an appreciative smile before looking to Xander. "You can totally find a replacement on Amazon."

"Is this a game to you?" Xander asks, voice unamused.

A smile treads carefully at the corner of my lips. "Most definitely." A soft burst of laughter erupts from the woman, and Xander lets out a sigh of frustration.

"Not helping, Zoelle."

"Sorry," she mumbles, biting her lip to keep from smiling or laughing. Probably both.

"It's alright," I chime in before Xander can continue, "I usually have that effect on people." I flutter my eyelashes enticingly at her and let my gaze sweep down her body.

"I didn't realize she was going to be as bad as you," bemoans Xander as he glares heartily at his brother. Ryatt is practically beaming at me, and I fight down the second wave of red that dares to rise. I just needed to outlast the effects of the tea. If that meant making a fool of myself and diverting attention accordingly, then so be it.

"Oh, she's a very bad girl," Ryatt claims proudly, his voice dipping dangerously low. "We've already discussed how we'll rectify the situation, haven't we,

Quinn?"

"Incorrigible," I growl, spearing him with a look of scorn. He sweeps my hand into his own and brings it to his lips.

"Always," he promises, teeth grazing my knuckles for the briefest of moments before retreating and allowing me back my hand. A shiver breaks out across my body as an almost undeniable urge to place my hand back within his own overwhelms me. A dull throbbing pulses from the back of my neck, near the base of my skull where a tattoo and birthmark call home. This had to be a side effect of the drug.

"Can we continue?" Xander asks, words laced with amusement and vexation. When no one answers, he leans back into his chair with a roll of his eyes. "I need a drink," he mutters just loud enough for us to hear.

"You should try the tea." Ryatt and Zoelle both snicker at Xander's groan. Then he straightens and pins his focus solely upon me.

"You stole the Wielding Crystal of Dan Furth," the woman, Zoelle, tells me. "It's an important artifact to my Coven." Coven, *right*.

"Who was your employer?" Xander asks. I shift uncomfortably in my seat.

"Mr. Vrana," I say after a painful moment's hesitation. The words burn a path on their way up and out my mouth. "Jesus Christ, how much of that *lunaria* stuff did you put in there? Can I have some water?"

Zoelle blushes. "It's probably because you drank it so fast," she explains to me patiently. "It'll fade. I

think. For now the effects will most likely feel
exacerbated."

"Perfect," I mutter.

"Quinn, focus." The glower I shoot Xander's way is
perfectly icy, as it should be. I've had enough practice
with it throughout my life. "Do you know who Mr.
Vrana is?"

"Just another man drooling over someone else's
toy."

"Do you know what he is?"

My eyes slip to Ryatt. "I've been told he's a
vampire."

"And do you believe him?" I flounder for an
answer, and my conflict gets stuck in my throat.

"I don't know," I finally say. "Not really, the
concept is pretty out there."

Xander nods and looks to Zoelle, his gaze softening
so much that he looks like a different man. *A man
terribly in love.* She reddens under his scrutiny but
returns his love-filled look.

"Rather disgusting, aren't they?" Ryatt asks softly,
effectively killing their mood. I snort.

"Yes," I respond resolutely.

"There's no need to be rude," Zoelle scolds Ryatt.
"After all, she's—" Zoelle cuts off at the precise
shaking of both brothers' heads.

"What? She's what?" I ask, scooting to the edge of
my seat and darting my gaze between the three.

"A thief," Ryatt answers, slowly turning to face me.
His face splits into a pleased grin. "Who stole my
heart."

Oh, Lord.

"You'll get used to it," Zoelle supplies at my incredulous look.

"I don't plan on having to," I tell her. My honesty places an uncomfortable look on their faces. "Am I missing something?"

"Only the important things," Ryatt answers. I'm ready to bite back, snap some witty retort to put him in his place when Xander holds up a hand.

"Would it help if one of us drank some of the tea?" I frown back at him. Why would he offer me that? As if reading my mind he replies, "So that you might believe. And so that you'll agree to help us get the crystal back." I sit back in my velvet chair carefully and slip one leg over the other.

"I want everyone to drink the tea."

He shakes his head. "Just one. You can choose." A sigh falls past my lips. There was no way for me to know if any of the trio had built up an immunity to the drug used in the tea. Meaning they could all potentially still lie to me and keep spinning this strange web of supernatural stories. I scan their faces briefly. If anyone seemed most likely to have built up an immunity to the drug, it was Xander. Ryatt would have too much fun being honest. Which left Zoelle.

"Her."

Zoelle straightens her shoulders a bit before pouring herself a cup of the now lukewarm tea. She drinks about half of it and then sets it down. *Smart.*

"It'll take a minute or so before the effects kick in," she explains to me, leaning against the desk as we all

72

wait out the minute in silence. "Alright. It should be working now."

"Good," Xander says. "Zoelle, what are you?"

"A witch," she says. I gaze on neutrally, ignoring the strong sound of my heart in my ears at her answer. Maybe she was a Wiccan. Wasn't that a religion? There's a long pause as all three turn expectant eyes towards me, but I refuse to pass along any sort of acknowledgment.

"And what are we?"

"You're lycans." *Not-werewolves.*

"And Mr. Vrana?" Her mouth opens then snaps shut as her face shifts to one of confusion.

"I've never met him. I wouldn't know. I *don't* know," comes her staggered response. Her hand grazes her throat as she clears it gently. A rather annoyed look flashing over her face.

"Sorry, love. I forgot you didn't know," Xander croons. "For the record, he's a vampire. And what does the crystal do?"

Zoelle takes a breath. "The crystal radiates a supernatural energy that stimulates the growth of the natural products of the land. It enhances their efficiency, potency, and power if they have it, tenfold. We already have one half," she tells me, "but Mr. Vrana, as you've told us, has the other." This was not good. Taking jobs knowing your employers are not quite right in the head always led to trouble.

"He might," I finally caution. "I don't know if he still has it. I mean," I grit my teeth against the uncomfortable sensation gripping my throat, "I am *nearly* certain he has it, but I can't know for sure. He made it seem like he wants it in his private collection. At least, somewhere out of reach of others."

"Do you believe us?" Zoelle asks uncertainly. My stomach twists unpleasantly.

"This is crazy!" I blurt out, "How can there be vampires and witches and lycans? How is this possible?"

"We all have our origins. Old gods and meddling spirits are typically the answer."

"Or witches hell-bent on revenge," Ryatt offers.

"We're not all bad," Zoelle grumbles.

"This is crazy," I mutter once more. My head is spinning with uncertain revelations. "And you want me to steal back this crystal from a *vampire*? A hypothetical supernatural creature that kills people by *drinking their blood*—are you nuts?!"

"You've already stolen it once from a lycan," Xander responds.

"I didn't know he was a lycan!" I snap back.

Zoelle shifts uncomfortably. "I know it's a lot to take in. When I was...brought into the fold, so to speak, it was a hard pill to swallow. I at least had my gran to help me adjust. This must be truly unbelievable to you."

Empathy coats her words, soothing the slow swell of distrust building inside of me. "Yeah," I hedge, "it is. Life isn't some television show or movie. Things like this just don't happen."

She chews on her lip, eyeing me speculatively before responding. "All I can say is that the sooner you accept it, the easier it will be to move forward. There's a lot more information and details to factor in when dealing with the supernatural. Trust me." She shoots a pointed glance at Xander, who sends her a mild frown in response.

"I'm not that bad."

I squeeze my eyes tightly shut and take several deep breaths. There were some pretty undeniable facts I needed to deal with immediately. One, I wasn't invincible. I had been caught. A trap had been neatly set, and I had fallen right into it. Two, I had been outsmarted. Plain and simple. The bruise to my ego would have to be nursed in private so that I could figure my way out of this mess. Three, an entire world had been hiding right under my nose. Lycans, witches, and vampires. Supposedly.

"Mr. Vrana…." his name tumbles from my mouth on an anxious breath, "he'll kill me. He's not the kind of man you cross and live to tell the tale. You have to understand. I just can't—"

"Quinn," Ryatt's voice breaks my tangent. It is laden with assurance and a dark undertone of possessiveness. "He is just one vampire going against an entire pack of wolves. Nothing will happen to you. I swear to you," he promises earnestly. My eyes slide open and turn to his steady gaze.

"I can't know that," I finally whisper. Vampire or not, Mr. Vrana was not a man to be crossed. This job wasn't worth my life. "I'm sorry, I—"

"I'm afraid we can't accept 'no' as an answer," Xander tells me, voice steady and unwavering. "If you don't help us we will be forced to alert the authorities of your presence and your past. All of which is on this flash drive." Xander picks up a USB drive from the side of his desk.

"You can't possibly—" I begin to protest, but his furious scowl quiets me.

"The Machon family heist, the Shorewood Cape Town scandal, the—" I hold up a hand and force my gaze to the ground, breathing harshly.

"How?" I look up to stare him down, and his eyes dart towards Ryatt. I let out a heavy sigh, feeling the weight of the world fall upon my shoulders. I was damned if I didn't, and damned if I did. *Fuck.* "Death or a jail cell," I ponder morosely, "I suppose I'll choose the jail cell." I don't bother trying to make eye contact with any of them, staring resolutely at the corner of the office instead.

"You'll be paid accordingly," Xander replies, "doubly so, of course." I remain silent.

"How about I take you to the kitchen and get you something real to eat?" Zoelle suggests after a moment. I nod stiffly and stand, shooting around the chair and heading to the door before either male can protest.

"Remember, Quinn," Ryatt calls over his shoulder, "don't do anything rash."

+++

Ryatt

"She's a bit of a handful, isn't she?" Xander asks, standing from behind his desk to pour us a drink.

"Isn't she glorious? All that fire and drive in one small package. She's smart too. She knows how to play the game. Knows how to control herself. The wolf is utterly smitten, and I'm infatuated," I admit, a lazy smile stretching across my face. "I couldn't have asked for a better soulmark. She's just like me, *but better.*"

Xander hands me my glass of bourbon. "She doesn't know about the soulmark, does she?"

I sip on my drink, enjoy its oaky flavor before responding. "No." But she knows I can bring her pleasure, unlike anything she's experienced before.

"Is that a good idea?" We catch each other's eye. Each assessing the other.

"I don't know," I mutter around the rim of my glass. "I just want her to like me for me."

My confession taints the air between us. I'm aware of the unusual streak of vulnerability I have laid bare before my Alpha and brother within the past week, but I can tell it brings us closer. I'm not the kind of wolf or man to share his feelings. In fact, I'm much more prone to acting in the moment and playing the crowd rather than letting on to my own emotions.

"I would rather not have our relationship, whatever it may be, revolve around it. I think we saw how tumultuous that could get." Another look is shared.

"True," Xander finally says, "but is kidnapping and blackmail any better? You're too reckless, Ryatt." I look away, the wolf and myself growing agitated. I shrug in response, not bothering to deny the

77

observation. It was true. I had a bad habit of jumping into things head first without looking, but wasn't finding your soulmark the perfect time to do just that? Granted, kidnapping and blackmail weren't exactly ideal ways of keeping one's soulmark by their side. But what other choice did I have now? Quinn was a thief, and one needed to catch a thief in order to have them.

CHAPTER 6

- Quinn -

The *lunaria* tea takes a long while to wear off. A fact Zoelle will not stop apologizing for, much to my annoyance. She rambles on and on, not letting me get a single word in as she fixes me the single best omelet I have ever eaten. By the time I finish the hearty breakfast, Zoelle has turned almost purple in the face. At least the *lunaria* had worn off.

She ushers me back to Ryatt's room, that monstrously sized man, Keenan, trailing slowly behind us. I don't take too much offense when the lock shutters and snaps into place behind me, or when Keenan is instructed quietly to stand guard. I do, however, take offense when I see my two Bric's suitcases and MCM weekender duffle nestled in the far corner of the room. I reach them in six large strides and kneel before them reverently.

These bags were my life. They were all I needed to get by. Clothes, shoes, toiletries, my encrypted laptop,

and a few precious mementos. They had been in my
car, ready and waiting for me to make my getaway. It
takes me an hour to go through all of them, carefully
cataloging every item to ensure nothing had been
taken.

Everything was there. Minus one thing: my laptop
charger. A quick check informs me that the laptop has
an 11% charge left. It wasn't a lot, but it could be just
enough to do *something*. Being forced to take the job
had left a bad taste in my mouth, and I was more
inclined at the moment to find a way out than to stay
and find a way to complete the job.

It's only after I'm done cataloging that I make a
thorough perusal of the room and all its exits. The
door was a no go, *obviously*. I tried the handle
experimentally only to be met with a predictable halt
as I attempt to turn the knob. Keenan's muted growl
was unneeded to demonstrate the point further. Even
if I could find the tools to pick the lock, he would still
be out there. *Asshat.* A look out the windows reveals
two other burly men standing below, casting the
occasional glance up as I peer out. A sound of
frustration boils in my chest. Scaling down the side of
the house would be difficult with two men on guard
and no trellis to guide me. I scour the room next,
looking for any sign of technology outside my laptop,
but find none.

"Right then," I mutter to myself. "Think, Quinn.
What next?"

I go back to my laptop and seat myself on the
ground. Priority number one was contacting Mr.

Vrana; or was it? If I pushed aside my pride and went through with the job, I'd be two million dollars richer. It would be more than enough to put in my off-shore accounts and live out my life somewhere far away from crazy vampires and lycans. And witches. I suppose I couldn't forget about those. I pinch the bridge of my nose before shaking my head in disbelief. What was I thinking? Those things didn't exist. Zoelle and Ryatt were just incredibly good liars. That had to be the reasoning for the shadow of doubt plaguing my conscious.

Priority number one would have to be finding records of my criminal past and wiping them clear. There was no need to find myself in this kind of situation again. Except I didn't have the juice to run that kind of search and removal on my laptop. A small smile finds its way onto my lips. Good thing I knew someone who could do it for me. I just needed to get them a message.

My laptop boots up normally, the screen a familiar black with flashes of green code zipping down its face. I enter in my credentials and locate the messaging interface I use with Big Bear, my contact. Just as I click the program, a message error occurs. I eye it warily and attempt to bypass it, but enough probing leads only to another message.

"What the—*no.*"

My eyes widen in horror and dread as a cartoon image of a shirtless Ryatt glides to the center of my screen, finger jutting out to waggle his finger at me.

"No, no, no," I hiss, frantically typing against the

virus that has been activated. The screen begins to go blurry at the edges before completely going black. "Fuck! Ugh!" I shut the laptop with an angry snap and flop backward, throwing an arm over my eyes rather dramatically. "God damn."

The lock clicks over several minutes later with the door easing open immediately after. The footfalls, though muted and light against the soft gray carpeting, are male. It wasn't Ryatt. The entrance would have been much grander and more demanding. Keenan was too big to move so gracefully as to make such little noise. Which meant...

"Go away, Xander," I grumble, not bothering to stray from my position of utter defeat. "Unless you've had a change of heart and have come to free me from my prison."

"I'm not Xander."

I remove my arm and sit up, a small frown burrowing its way into my brow as I stare at Keenan.

"How did you do that?" I ask seriously.

"I have the key," he responds dryly.

"Ha ha, very funny." His expression doesn't change, though I dare spy something akin to amusement in his eyes. "How did you move so quietly? You're a big guy." I outline his bulking shapes with my hands. "Guys your size, make way more noise, even when treading softly. Oh," my eyes alight with amusement, "is this a wolf thing?" I ask conspiratorially, flipping onto my stomach. "Wolves are sneaky, *ergo*—"

"No," he deadpans. Well, he wasn't any fun.

82

"Oh."

"Military," he corrects after a second of awkward staring and silence.

"Got it," I give him a thumbs up and flop back around, tossing my arm back in place to continue my wallowing. "What do you want, anyway?"

"I'm supposed to tell you that lunch will be brought to you at one. Dinner will be at seven downstairs, and..." I peek out to examine his strained delivery. He seems to be struggling with whatever it is he has to say, a bright pink straining up his neck to his ears. "Wear something to show off your beautiful bust and magnificent ass, darling."

We stare at each other in mild horror before I give a strangled laugh. "Excuse you?"

"Ryatt's words, not mine," he all but growls and stomps out of the room. The door shudders with the force of his exit, and the lock slides determinedly into place. It starts to happen again. A tiny, absolutely minuscule, smile tugging at the corner of my lips. *That idiot.* How he got the enormous man to comply would most likely remain a mystery, but at least it had been entertaining, and somehow, it had felt like an apology.

+++

I have several dresses packed away in my luggage, all carefully rolled within tissue paper and placed next to a mini portable garment steamer. I choose my outfit carefully, Ryatt's words haunting me. He wanted a dress to show off my figure? *Fine.* But his wouldn't be

the only head turning tonight. The Elizabeth and
James Rosa Dress is extremely flattering with its
asymmetrical hemline and V-neckline that plunges
just enough. The navy blue crepe dress is set off with
gold cuffs and hoop earrings. I look a vision, if I do say
so myself. I tug at the base of my ponytail to tighten it,
overseeing my movements in the bathroom mirror
with a critical eye.

No one had bothered me the rest of the day,
leaving me to find my amusements in the books
strewn about the room and photographs on the wall.
Mostly though, I had been working out my next move.
I would help the Adolphus family get their precious
crystal back, then get the hell out of dodge.

The best time to get back the crystal would be
during the art premiere that Mr. Vrana was hosting. I
would go, and under cover of the masses, swipe the
crystal and replace it with a fake. Hopefully, by the
time he realized he was no longer in possession of the
real crystal, I would be long gone. Untraceable.
Forgotten.

A knock sounds at the door just as I finish
touching up my lipstick. *Show time.* I give myself a
final look over, smoothing my hair and examining my
choice of eye shadow. My Steve Madden stilettos are
the finishing touch to my ensemble, but I linger in
front of the mirror before putting them on. I could do
this. So what if my whole world had just been turned
upside down? This was just another job. And each job
came with new rules and different players. *I could do
this.*

The door to the bedroom opens, accompanied by a second knock to alert me to their presence.

"Ready?" Ryatt calls. With a forlorn sigh, I give myself a mental shake. I walk out of the bathroom and over to the foot of the bed where my stilettos await me. "You look...dazzling."

His voice sounds full of amazement. Awe, even, but I force myself not to look at him. Instead, I remain focused on the art of slipping into my heels without twisting an ankle.

"Ready," I say, plastering a demure smile on my lips. Ryatt clears his throat and holds out his arm, giving me his own charming smile.

"Shall we then?" My fingers grace the soft linen of his suit jacket.

"Hugo Boss?"

Ryatt's eyes twinkle down at me as he leads me from the room. "Burberry."

"They have excellent slim-cut suits," I tell him matter-of-factly, taking on a new persona: *Alice*. Fashion connoisseur and full of worldly culture. Much like myself, I think with a self-satisfied smirk.

"Looking forward to dinner?" Ryatt asks, the barest hint of reluctance in his voice as he watches my face.

"If Zoelle is making it, I am," I tell him honestly. Lunch had been a green gazpacho soup with a whole grain roll on the side. She had even left a note on the tray, asking if I had any allergies. Thank God I didn't, lest I tamper with her divine cooking skills.

"She is," Ryatt confides as he leads me down a

rather grandiose staircase. My eyes flit across the expanse of the room, narrowing in on the potential routes of escape should things take a turn for the worse. It was always good to keep one's options open. "She has her own little patisserie and café, as it would happen. It's doing very well so far, but it's no surprise. She's quite *magical* in the kitchen."

I roll my eyes as we finish our descent. "That was horrible."

"That was funny," he insists gaily.

"It wasn't," I deadpan. "You're basically a grown child."

"I don't think children come quite as equipped as I do," he tells me innocently, "or do you require a refresher?"

"Are you ever serious?" I complain, slipping my hand from the crook of his elbow. I needed to be on my A-game tonight, and our little tête-à-tête was distracting. Each quip felt like a subtle poke at my carefully constructed wall. Searching out my weak points. I hadn't forgotten his little proposition in the hallway. *A chance to explore what could be between us?* My heart skips a beat at his earlier words. *Yeah, right.* He catches me before I can storm off, pulling me flush against him. Goodness, his eyes were blue. Like the sky on a perfect summer's day. Endless and stunning in their clarity.

"I'm serious about wanting you," he tells me solemnly, all traces of humor fleeing. My mouth goes slack at his confession, and I flounder under his heated gaze. He smiles then, softly and small. "Too much?" he jokes and goes about putting my hand back to where it was, leading me once again to the dining room. "I'm afraid I only run on two systems: lighthearted or intense. You'll find that my siblings run on a similar system. Xander is either brooding or intense and Irina either tender or haughty. Xander usually falls to the former. Irina the latter."

"Good to know," I mutter, calming my speeding heart with slow, deep breaths.

"Nervous?"

I scoff, rolling back my shoulders and knocking my head up a fraction. "Hardly."

"Just wait till you meet Irina," he replies back cheerily enough, then stops in front of a set of doors. He sends me an assessing look, back to serious mode. "You'll do fine in there," he assures me.

"I didn't realize I had anything to be nervous about. This is just a business dinner. I'm here on business." Ryatt takes a second before nodding curtly in response and opening the door. Time for *Charlotte Donovan* to make her appearance. The perfectly posh dinner guest to end all dinner guests. Ready to handle all manner of snobbery thrown her way.

Everyone is seated: Xander, Zoelle, and a raven-haired woman who must be Irina. I meet each pair of eyes with a cool look, pleased to see Xander look uncomfortably away and Zoelle turn red.
Unfortunately, the last of the party doesn't react as I had hoped. Her eyes, a startling green against her fair skin, appraise me with apparent displeasure. As if I am gum stuck on the bottom of one of her shoes. Her

disdain is nothing Charlotte Donovan can't handle.

"Good evening, everyone," greets Ryatt, ushering me into the seat next to Zoelle. Ever the gentleman, he pulls out my chair and pushes me in, claiming the seat next to his sister and opposite me.

"I like your dress," Zoelle compliments.

I give her a somewhat strained smile in return, then turn my gaze to Irina, who has yet to finish her appraisal. "Is that a Fallon necklace?" Irina's eyes alight with a semblance of approval.

"It is," she replies, her voice smooth as silk. "It's from the Armure Collection. That's quite the eye you have, though; I suppose when one makes a living off of stealing fine goods they're bound to learn a thing or two about quality."

Point Irina. My smile tightens. Zoelle clears her throat at the standstill.

"So," she hedges awkwardly, "you steal for a living. How do you enjoy your work?" Irina's eyebrows nearly clear her hairline at the question, but mine are a close second. Ryatt clears his throat, amusement written clearly over his face at Zoelle's crude remark. Then his eyes dart pointedly to me and I put on a more diplomatic look.

"I like to think of myself as a property re-investor."

"That's quite catchy," Ryatt remarks, raising his wine glass in salute to me. "Don't you think so, Irina? Xander?"

"That's one way to put it, I suppose," Xander agrees. He seems to be suffering from secondhand embarrassment on his significant other's account.

"A thief is a thief," Irina comments, her tone suggesting she will not be swayed from her viewpoints. "At least you're doing it in style," she says after a moment, her tone not exactly softening, but becoming warmer. "I have the Rosa Dress in Raspberry Ice."

I relax my posture just slightly and meet her piercing gaze. "Not many people can pull off that color."

She smiles loftily. "I know." Ryatt shoots me an approving look that has me biting my tongue. As if I need his approval. Out of the corner of my eye, I see Zoelle pass Xander a somewhat helpless look.

"Ryatt told me you have a café?" A plate of mini tuna tartare's is placed before each of us; little crostini displayed around the spherical mound in a semi-circle. I wonder how Zoelle's would compare to La Menagerie's.

"Yes," she answers proudly, "I opened it just a month or two ago. I've had a good profit so far, but that's because I worked like a dog to promote it beforehand." I'm about to dig into the tasty first course when my fork stalls, as if by its own accord.

"This wouldn't happen to be laced with any kind of, I don't know, weird, magical drug, would it?"

"Oh! No!" Zoelle cries in distress, "Absolutely not, no. Here, take mine." She swaps our plates before I can protest and takes a rather hearty bite of the dish as if to prove her honesty. Irina looks on in unveiled disgust at Zoelle's performance before rolling her eyes and digging in herself. Ryatt looks to be holding back a laugh and Xander is once more taken under by secondhand embarrassment. I had a feeling that was going to be happening a lot to him tonight.

The tartare is delectable, cool, and refreshing. And, dare I say, even better than La Menagerie? "Did you make this?" I ask.

"No," she says, the stain of her blush still rampant on her cheeks. "I did make the menu for tonight though, and outlined the recipes for the household kitchen staff to go by."

Everyone enjoys the rest of the first course in relative silence until all plates are wiped neatly clean of any remaining crumbs. Course two comes out, a small, spiral tower of what looks to be pasta carbonara. *Mmm.*

"Do you cook?" Xander asks politely.

"I make a mean toast," I tell him seriously, "and I've been known to prepare an equally formidable bag of chips."

"A woman after my own heart," Ryatt comments, taking a slow drink of his wine as he watches me once more with that heated gaze.

"Don't listen to him," Irina rebuffs. "He's always so sensational."

I smirk, "I hadn't noticed." Our dinner continues, and I'm surprised by the relative peace that is kept. I suppose that meant it was time to shake things up a bit. "So," I begin as my empty plate is taken away and my glass of wine refilled. "I've learned about lycans from Ryatt. A bit here and there about witches thanks to Zoelle. What should I know about vampires?"

There's an edge to my cordial tone—a mix between patronizing and condescending skepticism.

My dinner company shares measured looks. Xander seems as if he is about to begin but looks to Ryatt instead, as if to give him the right-of-way to explain. Which is when Irina speaks up.

"They're quite vain creatures," she tells me matter-of-factly. "Though, much of that has to do with preserving their bodies. They are dead after all. The supplement of blood from others, humans and animals alike, is a tricky thing. You see, as vampires get older, more blood is required to keep their bodies in pristine condition. The larger intake also helps evolve and strengthen their supernatural abilities of speed and strength. The oldest vampires can even compel others to do their will. It's a bit like hypnosis, I suppose." She trails off with a far-off look in her eyes until quickly shaking herself of her reverie.

"New vampires are rarely made, as their bloodlust in the first 50 years or so is so unstable. Many succumb to the bloodlust if not taken under the guidance of their sire, becoming slaves to their hunger and running rampant like mongrels."

"Does that mean they're extremely fast and strong during those fledgling years if they're consuming large amounts of blood?"

Irina cuts into her roasted chicken thigh delicately. "Indeed, they are. They're quite the nuisance to kill. Which is done through beheading, of course."

I nod my head along decisively as if this can be the only reasonable answer. *Of course.* "What else?"

91

"They're typically very cold to the touch unless they have a Heart Stone ring. It's a magical item that warms the wearer's internal body temperature. Silver eyes—well, not at the beginning. As vampires age, the more silver their eyes appear. It's an easy way to estimate how old a vampire is. Those that are a few hundred years old will have distinctive silver streaks in their irises, whereas a fledgling might only have a ring about the iris. The ancients are completely turned. It's quite unnerving if you ask me.

"Let's see, what else. *Ah!* They don't fare well under direct sunlight. The UV rays promote the aging process, and their skin begins to flake off. It's very grotesque. Several members of the ancient families possess rings known as the Amethysts of the Aztecs. They allow the wearer to walk in the daylight without falling harm under the sun."

Fascinating. They really did believe the stories they told. "If lycans are children of the moon and were then cursed by a witch, how were vampires created?"

"A witch," Ryatt supplies.

"No," Irina corrects condescendingly, fork and knife paused mid-cut. "A necromancer. The last of the necromancers to be precise. Between 1186 and 1207, necromancers were hunted down and exterminated. Necromancers draw on dark magic to resurrect the dead, but also draw power from each other. As their numbers became smaller and smaller, so did the reach of their power.

"The necromancer who brought about the vampire line was Nicholas Vogart. He used all of his powers to

bring back his dead lover, Regulus. Except Regulus
had been dead for more than two weeks," she tells me
surreptitiously, a devious smirk on her face. "Well, it
is well known that the longer a person is dead, the
harder it is to reanimate them. Yet, here comes
Nicholas, an unusually powerful necromancer and the
last known of his kind, using all the power he
possesses to resurrect his dead lover. But—"

"Wait! How did he die?"

"Who?"

"Regulus," I say with some amount of
exasperation. I cannot help but be enraptured by her
story. She speaks it as she would some juicy gossip.

Irina's cheeks take on a delicate rosy hue.
"Dysentery," she supplies. "Anyway, back to the story.
Nicholas is able to reanimate his lover, but according
to lore, the use of such a powerful spell weakened
Nicholas gravely. He fell to his knees before the
reanimated corpse and began to weep tears of blood.
Whether they were tears of joy or pain are uncertain,
though it is more than likely it was a combination of
both. Regulus took to his knees in a mirror image of
his creator, feeling an unfamiliar pang resounding in
his dead heart. Slowly, carefully, he reached out to
wipe away Nicholas's tears. Then Regulus brought his
fingers to his lips and licked away the blood." Irina
snaps her fingers dramatically. "Instantly he was
changed! No longer was he an animated corpse, but
truly brought back to life by his lover's tears and
blood. Consumed by the taste, he fell upon Nicholas
like a wild animal and drained him of his blood."

"Holy shit," I breathe, traces of plain old Quinn coming through. "That is really cool." How had Ryatt gotten everyone to go along with his supernatural narrative?

"It is a gripping origin, but you must always remember they're ruthless creatures. If ever in doubt, think on Regulus, who could not control his thirst. Yes," she continues with a sigh, "they're very proud and very smart creatures, but when one can live forever, it's not so surprising."

"How do you know all of this?" Xander asks, his face adorably scrunched in confusion.

"I do read, you know," she huffs, tossing her hair over her shoulders. I roll back my shoulders and slip back into *Charlotte Donovan.*

"Thanks for all the information. Besides speed and strength, do they have any other supernatural abilities? Enhanced hearing or seeing? If I'm going to steal from some hundred-year-old vampire, I need to know."

"How silver are his eyes?" Ryatt asks.

"Enough. Though, it doesn't come off as too unnatural since they're already such a pale blue."

"What's your plan?" Xander asks.

"I'll attend the artist premiere next week at his home and crack his safe. He made it seem like he would keep it close, so I assume it's there. If I could reach out to some of my contacts I'd be able to confirm." I swing my gaze to Ryatt who smiles innocently back. "It would also be easier if someone would return my laptop charger and remove the virus from my laptop."

"I happen to know a fantastic hacker. Best in the field," Ryatt confides. Dessert is placed before us, some chocolate treat that I ignore.

"Best?" I scoff. "Slipping a virus onto someone's computer isn't exactly hard."

Ryatt's returning grin bites, "Careful darling, you'd do well not to wound my pride. You can use any one of our computers—"

"No," I interrupt, "my contacts, my rules. We use my laptop, or we go in blind and hope for the best." The room practically vibrates with tension.

"That seems reasonable," Zoelle whispers to Xander. I shoot her a grateful look.

"It is, isn't it?"

"Fine," Ryatt gets out, "I'll remove the virus, and you can work on your laptop, but you'll be supervised. We don't want you doing anything that would stir unwanted attention."

I stifle my retort and take a drink of wine instead. Setting it down neatly, I fold my hands in my lap before I reply. "Fine." *Point to Ryatt.*

"I'll also accompany you to the event."

"What?" I glare at Ryatt and pass an incredulous look to his brother. "No deal. He'll give me away."

"Surely you need a date for the event. I've been known to be quite the arm candy."

"Won't Mr. Vrana know you're a lycan?"

"Unlikely," Irina interjects, finishing off her chocolate tart. "Unless we are caught displaying our abilities, then we cannot be identified by scent. Not by a vampire anyway."

"I work alone," I say curtly, "in case I have to partake in more...illicit activities to gain what I need."

Ryatt growls from across the table, his eyes flashing that strange gold. "I will accompany you," he tells me, voice filled with unrestrained possessiveness. "End of discussion."

Plain old Quinn rears her head, not liking one bit the way he takes charge with another decision that should be left to me. "It's just business, Ryatt. No need to take it so personally," I respond overly sweetly.

"I'd say our night in Mexico was personal," he retorts, leaning forward. "Based on your reactions during our...business...I'd say you found our transaction more than personal as well."

"Enough!" Xander shouts, his voice anchored in authority. My mouth shuts with a snap. As does Ryatt's. "Quinn, you'll work with your contacts to discern the location of the crystal and make a plan of action. Ryatt will monitor your work and accompany you to the artist premiere. That's final." *Point Xander.*

I cannot contain the angry scowl that works its way onto my features. Having a partner was unnecessary. He would only slow me down. Moreover, it was an insult. I could accomplish the mission by myself, easily.

I take a deep, calming breath, envisioning in my mind's eye causing some serious damage to Ryatt's face with my fist. My muscles loosen at the thought, a satisfied smile coming across my face.

"Thinking of something pleasant, are we?" he asks

rakishly.

"Only of digging your grave," I respond sweetly. "Any place you want to be buried?"

Ryatt smirks back at me. "*Inside you.*"

"Oh honestly, Ryatt!" Irina shrieks.

"Were we this bad at the start?" Zoelle asks Xander quietly. "I thought the soulmark was supposed to make you like the other person?"

"Not exactly. It can certainly warm you to a person, but it doesn't force you to like them. It's just that the soulmark is your other half—why wouldn't you fall for them?" he replies back softly.

"This does not seem like a warm reception," she whispers back. Zoelle catches my questioning gaze and colors.

"What's a soulmark?" The room comes to a standstill, each face carrying varying amounts of worry. Oh no.

"*Thanks,*" Ryatt sighs, then downs the rest of his wine.

CHAPTER 7
– Quinn –

Belle Creations is much nicer inside than the displays in the window lead one to believe on the outside. It has a cool modern edge, and their products are placed in precise lines with an obvious flow of formality. Since the artist premiere is a black tie affair, we head towards the back to select a range of gowns for me to try on. Zoelle picks three. Irina seven. The shopping attendants send us to the private back room for me to try on the gowns, while Irina and Zoelle are seated in over-stuffed chairs covered in chaste pink to make their critiques. Sparkling white wine soon follows after I come out in the first dress, much to my pleasure. At least this small town knew how to luxe it up.

I take my time putting on the first dress; my mind stuck on last night's events. Dinner had turned into a very confusing explanation of what a "soulmark" was and the implications of Ryatt having already sealed it.

After all was said and done, I felt myself still choking on anger from the way Ryatt proved the soulmarks existence at the dinner table. Reaching out, he had clasped his hand around the back of my neck. Our foreheads brushing together as I let out a strangled moan from the brief touch. It had been completely unnecessary and embarrassing. Yet his behavior at dinner was downright pleasant when compared to his behavior after

+++

"I can't believe you!" I seethe, marching towards Ryatt's bedroom. "Here I thought I was the one taking advantage of you—"

"—You were."

"—and then you just go ahead and condemn me to some supernatural life sentence!" My feet hasten towards the bedroom door, guiding me inside the room with quick steps so I might turn and slam the door in his face—the least of which he deserves. Of course, his hand shoots out before I can get it even halfway closed, his face a mixture of frustration and agony.

"Just let me explain," he pleads, pushing inside after me and shutting the door with a soft push.

"I think everything was explained just fine at dinner," I tell him, fire scorching my words. "Don't think this little revelation changes the way I feel about you. Which—to be clear—is nothing but absolute loathing."

Ryatt looks somewhat aghast. "But Mexico—"

99

"Ugh! Mexico was just a job, Ryatt. You and the stupid crystal were just another paycheck. Okay? It meant nothing. I played a role and I played you. That's it."

"Don't tell me it meant nothing," he all but growls. "It might have been a job, but there was something real there that night before the soulmark was discovered. At the bar we were tit for tat. We both knew we were playing a game, but we appreciated how well the other played it. I don't give a damn if you say it was some role you played, I saw you that night. Past your little facade. Past all the ones you keep trying to put up. There was something real between us that night. How can you deny the chemistry we had? Have."

"No! There was no chemistry. There is no chemistry. No 'we.'"

"For Christ's sake, Quinn. You house the other half of my soul. Of course there's something between us. Sealing the soulmark simply sparked something more inside of each of us. A connection that demands to be acknowledged. A craving and desire."

My breath stalls, a damnable vise stealing down upon my heart at his impassioned words. His words ring true; at least, this is what my heart begs me to believe. I think on how desperately it wants love. Then remember all the times in the past when it has been denied. I know better than to believe pretty words from beautiful men.

"More like disgust and revulsion," I finally choke

out.

He pinches the bridge of his nose and takes a deep breath, letting it out in a sharp exhalation. Ryatt gives a humorless laugh, taking a step forward. His eyes smolder with wicked intent. "If you recall, the soulmark also conjures feelings of absolute, all-consuming pleasure. Are you really trying to tell me you didn't feel it tonight? What about back in Mexico? Or are you usually that enthusiastic about sucking one of your targets off?"

I match his step with a heated glare, a flush of rage spreading across my body. It lights me up from inside out. "So what if I did? The fact still remains; you had no right to seal the stupid mark without me knowing! To condemn me to a life with you or go crazy!"

"I had every right! You're my soulmark. My soul mate! Mine," he growls.

Ryatt's eyes spill gold leaving not a single trace of familiar blue behind. It's the wolf, my heart tells me, though my head still dares to deny it. The gold seeps back, leaving a stormy blue in their wake. The man placed back in charge.

"If our souls are meant to be one, who am I to ignore it?" Ryatt tells me in a measured cadence. "True, our sealing was not ideal. Nor was it considerately done, but it was obviously more than necessary seeing as you drugged *me, then left me for* dead.*"*

Ugh. A sneer curls its way onto my lip. "Your sister is right; you are sensational. I didn't leave you

101

for dead. You were fine by morning."

Ryatt closes the distance between us, his face inches from mine. A shiver runs across my skin. I credit the action to my anger, but the soulmark dares to suggest otherwise as it thrums against my skin. I bite back a groan of disbelief, steeling myself against the sudden rush of desire flooding through my veins. Why did this happen every time he was within reach? This damnable soulmark was going to be the death of me. Or Ryatt, considering how badly I wished to throttle him.

Or maybe it would take us both under.

"I'll have you know most women would be ecstatic about finding their literal soul mate, not to mention that it's me—"

"God! Get over yourself! As if you're God's gift to women."

Lightning strikes between us. The tension finally comes to a rupture as Ryatt cups my chin and brands me with his kiss. I'm pressed against the window before I can blink, hips pinned in place by his own as my hands tangle themselves into his hair. Something like electricity runs rampant over me. Leaves me aching with the most terrible want. Hands spread themselves across my sides, trailing up my arms before landing on my breasts. We both let out a moan, eyes opening to meet in our haze of anger-induced lust.

His blue eyes are streaked with amber, and they look down at me with clear intent: ravage. His fingers pinch at my nipples, and I give a startled cry. One he

*happily consumes, mouth pressing against mine
brutally again as I rock my hips forward. A hand
inches slowly upwards to my neck and I feel my skin
burn in anticipation. With a heady rock of his hips, he
earns another moan.*

*The edges of the soulmark yearn for his touch—
almost painfully so. There is no chance of ignoring the
steady beat it raps against the back of my neck and
the accompanying symphony of shivers its sends
across my body.*

*"I want you to remember this," he whispers in my
ear, tongue swiping out to taste it. "Remember the
pleasure. The ecstasy of it all, and know that I could
give you so much more. If you'd only dare give me a
chance."*

*His words stutter on a choke, blue eyes gazing into
mine with uncertain trust. And then his fingers find
the soulmark and I am lost in a spiral of sensation.
Ryatt's hips buck into mine, a strangled growl
sounding in my ear as he yanks one leg up and around
his waist. My dress rides up uncomfortably around my
hips, but it only leaves the faintest of impressions
when compared to the kaleidoscope of feelings
careening through my body. Every nerve ending comes
alive, standing to attention at the call of such rapt
pleasure. It makes my blood sing. My heart soar.*

*"Oh God," I cry, hips pushing relentlessly against
Ryatt's as my hands claw at his body. What was this?
How could the soulmark make me feel so...good? So
wickedly good and oh so satisfied. Every man before
Ryatt quickly falls to the wayside as I feel a deeper*

*pull bringing us together. "Please," I whimper. His
hand slips from the soulmark, and I give a cry of
despair before replacing it with one of relief.*

*A brief pinching against the skin of my thighs and
my panties are ripped from my body, his hand neatly
taking their place. Ryatt's eyes dilate as he finds me
soaking with excitement. When his mouth finally seals
back over mine, he pushes two fingers inside me.*

*"Tell me," he asks after a minute of kissing me
breathless. He inserts another finger, watching as my
body contracts with pleasure. "Tell me it means
nothing." My eyes snap open to meet his, lips forming
an "O" as I am ripped away from my pleasure haze.*

*"What?" When I make no other reply he slowly
begins to extract himself—fingers slipping out of me,
his hand dropping my thigh. Ryatt takes two steps
back, a growing frown upon his face. No.*

"Tell me it means nothing and I'll leave."

*"Are you fucking serious?" My body trembles with
the threat of release.*

*Eyes still locked on mine, he brings each glistening
finger one by one to his mouth to lick them clean.
"Very. I want to hear you say it again. That there is no
chemistry between us. That there is nothing at all
between us. Soulmark or not."*

*"Fuck you," I spit, surprised to find myself near
tears. Ryatt's nostrils flare.*

*"So be it. I'll sleep elsewhere tonight. If you decide
to accept the truth, to accept me, I'll gladly finish what
we started." My eyes flit across the room, landing on a
framed photo atop a side table. It shatters against the*

wall near the door as he makes his exit.
  "Bastard."

+++

Irina's head tilts to the side in assessment before shaking her head. "I don't like it. You need something with a bit more flow for the skirt, don't you think? To conceal the supplies."

I barely have the curtain pulled back before Irina makes her comment. Zoelle's face falls slightly. I turn and look at myself in the mirror.

"I think you're right," I murmur.

"Obviously," she scoffs. I grab five of the dresses, all form-fitting, and pass them to an attendant.

"We won't be needing these," I tell her with a smile. Irina shoots me an angry pout but says nothing more, even though all five dresses are her picks.

"You do realize this means we'll be getting home much sooner than originally planned? Ryatt is probably wearing a hole in one of the Turkish runners as we speak. Pacing like some mother hen, waiting for your return."

"Doubtful," I call from inside the dressing room, slipping out of the black evening gown and into a red one.

"Is this about the fight you had last night?" Irina asks.

Zoelle gives a light gasp, "Oh no, you two fought?"

"How the hell did you know we fought?" I bluster, struggling with the side zipper.

105

"You weren't exactly quiet," she replies defensively.

"I thought everyone was still downstairs having their nightcaps."

"We were," Zoelle explains. "Would you bring us some water? Thanks." Quick steps tread from the private dressing room. The other attendant, no doubt. "They hear, like, everything."

I pause and catch myself frowning in the mirror. "That's annoying," I whisper under my breath. There is a moment's hesitation where I wait expectantly for Irina's cool comeback, but hearing none, I smile and step out of the dressing room with a flourish.

"It's just as annoying for us as it is for you. Do you think I want to hear you being groped by my brother, or you," Irina directs a pointed glare at Zoelle, "having at it with my other brother." She lets out a plaintive sigh. "I have to move out."

"Can't you just turn it off?"

"It's not as simple as that, unfortunately."

Zoelle takes a sip from the champagne flute, eyeing me cautiously over it. "Just ask me," I snip.

"Why were you fighting?"

"Why else would we be fighting? The soulmark, obviously." Irina holds up her hand for silence, and the attendant walks in a few moments later holding a tray with three glasses of water.

"Thank you, that will be all for now," Irina tells the shop attendant without a second glance. The woman nods.

"Just ring the bell if you ladies need anything

more," she tells us, then walks back to the front of the shop.

"Is it because he sealed the mark without your permission?" Zoelle asks cautiously.

"Yes!" I cry, turning on my heel and heading back into the dressing room. "For whatever reason, he can't seem to wrap his head around the concept that sealing the soulmark was not his decision to make alone." I tug and tug at the zipper to no use and stomp my foot. "Would one of you—"

The curtain pulls back to reveal Irina, her vibrant green eyes swirling with emotion. She hands me my glass of sparkling wine and fiddles with the zipper. It acquits to her persuasion.

"You're right," she says carefully, "but you're both guilty of wrongdoings that night." She coerces the zipper down as I finish off the glass of sparkling wine in two unladylike swallows.

I give a little nod, passing the flute back to her, my hands awkwardly holding the dress to my body. "Ryatt changed the entire course of my life with his decision," I tell them flatly, memories of my less than stellar childhood simmering to the surface. I had grown used to making my own choices and decisions young, both easy and hard. I didn't need anyone else doing it for me now. A rasp of laughter falls from my lips before I continue. "I have every right to be mad."

"So there's no hope you'll forgive him?" Irina asks sadly. My heart gives a little quiver at the thought.

"Xander and I had a rough start as well," Zoelle continues, standing up to join our small gathering.

107

"Actually, it was Ryatt who saw my soulmark first and brought Xander into the picture."

"Ah yes, the little tête-à-tête in the forest," Irina murmurs.

"Ryatt chased me down with Keenan and Dominic, both in their wolf forms." Wolf forms? I hold back my eye roll then cock my head to the side.

"Did they put you in the creepy family dungeon?" Both women color.

"No, but I was tied up rather savagely. Xander sealed the mark without my having a clue as to what was going on. I had no idea I was a witch and had no explanation for what I had witnessed in the woods. My entire world was flipped. I was scared and angry, but I was also...intrigued. There was a pull tugging at my very core towards Xander that I couldn't escape. After a while, I didn't want to ignore it."

"He wouldn't let you ignore it," Irina corrects.

Zoelle gives a short shrug, "I think it was a bit of both. It wasn't exactly smooth sailing after we completed the soulmark. We had a lot of things to work out, but after a lot of talks—"

"—and a lot of sex."

Zoelle blushes, "—we were able to find a happy place."

"By 'happy place', she means they are annoyingly happy. All the time." Irina tells me candidly. "Isn't that what you want? Isn't that what everyone wants? Love? Disgusting, nauseatingly sweet love?"

I guffaw, "Don't you think it's weird that some cosmic force has split your soul and placed the other half in your 'soul mate.' Then doesn't even guarantee you find them? And when you do—*if you do*—your whole life suddenly reroutes to revolve around this one person, and if you resist...you go crazy. That's fucked up."

Irina huffs. "It's 'fucked up' to you because you're just a human. Soulmarks are well known in the supernatural community. For us, finding our soulmark is like skipping the whole awkward dating phase."

"What part of having your life turn upside down is not awkward?"

"It's called love, Quinn. Honestly, there's no need to be such an old shrew about it."

"I am not an old shrew!" I shriek.

"You guys, would you calm down?" Zoelle gently pushes me back inside the dressing room to finish changing. "Irina—"

"I'm only trying to be helpful," she whines. "Why none of you can see that is beyond me. I thought gaining a sister meant having someone to take my side, Zoelle. But you're just as bad as Xander. Maybe being Alpha has gone to your head."

"Don't be so dramatic," I say, slipping the blue gown on.

"It's a family thing," Zoelle sighs. Irina makes a noise of protest.

"Excuse you," she rebuffs. "Here I am, once again trying to mend bridges on behalf of my brother, and what do I get? Impudence? Unbelievable! I'll have you know, Zoelle, you're just as stubborn as Xander. And you!" The curtain yanks open and I give a small yelp. Irina's finger points accusingly at me, "Are just as bad, if not worse, than Ryatt with your theatrics. Don't think for a moment you two aren't meant for each other. *Honestly.*"

Irina crosses her arms over her chest while Zoelle and I stare back at her, mouths agape.

"So dramatic," I say, shaking my head lightly. Zoelle lets out a giggle, one that is dangerously contagious until all of us unravel in a fit of laughter. Catching my breath, I give a twirl, the chiffon flaring out. Point to Zoelle and me.

"I think I'll get this one."

+++

As shopping hadn't taken nearly as long as Irina anticipated, we go for a late lunch at some American-French bistro and stick around for happy hour. Of course, I am easily able to persuade Irina into continuing our certified "girls' day" into a "girls' night." Irina, in turn, is able to guilt Zoelle into continuing as well. Which is why when we return around midnight—very much intoxicated—I begin to hiccup from the butterflies flying around my stomach.

Not that I had any reason to be nervous. Chances were slim that Ryatt was even in the bedroom. Chances were—my eyes alight with sudden hope—I could make my getaway!

Hiccup.

My drunken knees wobble as I dip into an uneasy

110

crouch, arms out to balance myself. *Stupid heels.* My eyes skirt nervously from left to right, doubling back when I see a shadowed figure at the end of the hallway. I let out a quick shriek, but a hand is even quicker to clamp over my mouth. Wide-eyed, I stare in alarm at Keenan and his ever-present frown.

"Don't do that," I whisper-yell at him once his hand is removed. "I could have had a heart attack!"

"You should go to bed," he suggests, humor tinging his voice. My eyes narrow upon him.

"You're not my mother," I tell him with a sneer, poking his chest to drive my point home.

Keenan gives pause. "Bed," he deadpans, taking a step forward, all pleasantness dropping. Point to Keenan. I let out a small *"eep"* and launch myself inside the bedroom, slamming the door behind me. Lord, that man was frightening, but at least he got rid of my hiccups.

"You're back late," Ryatt says, signature smirk in place as he exits the ensuite bathroom. He is bathed in light, steam slowly billowing out of the doorway around him. I gulp nervously, butterflies fluttering into a frenzy at the sight.

Stay cool, Quinn. "...Yep."

"How was your night?"

Good, I think to myself. *Better than expected.*

I had never had real girlfriends growing up. Never a mother to confide in. M was the closest thing I had, but all she had ever taught me to do was steal hearts and money. M's influence had been quite clear tonight, as I drunkenly attempted to swipe both Irina and

111

Zoelle's phones and wallets some point after Mai Tai number four. Old habits die hard, I guess.

Yet, rather than be mad, they had laughed at my drunken attempts and scolded me, attempting to persuade me from my life of crime with promises of Zoelle's delicious cooking and a free pass to Irina's closet. It was a tempting offer, with the underlying promise of sisters and a large family encompassed in their words. Their playful yet sincere nature had done a number on the wall around my heart, leaving it battered and bruised. And a tad too vulnerable for my liking.

"It was a good time," I tell him, cringing as my words slur at the end.

His eyes widen in delight, running a towel over his hair briskly, muscles rippling enticingly at the simple action. "Are you drunk?" he asks casually, though I most certainly detect traces of humor to it. Much like Keenan.

"No." My head shakes firmly, side to side, causing an uncomfortable wave of dizziness to overcome me. Maybe I should take off my heels? "Definitely not," I reply smoothly, no trace of a slur to my words whatsoever. "Super sober girl over here." Yep, that was me: *super sober Sophie.* She was a new character to add to my collection.

"Is that so?" He tosses the towel carelessly behind him onto the bathroom floor and readjusts the one around his waist.

"Why are you all wet? I mean—" a swell of heat rushes to my face "—why are you taking a shower. At

112

midnight?"

"I was patrolling the borders with a few others. Without the full power of the crystal, we have to take extra precautions. Ergo, running longer patrols in larger packs."

"Uh huh."

My eyes watch as the few remaining water droplets make their way down his pectorals and sculpted abs. Why did he have to be so good looking? Everything about him was the epitome of lithe and dangerous. Absolutely sinful. And he knew it. Worse still, he knew I knew it. I chew on my lower lip, gazing at his torso thoughtfully as I toe off my heels.

It wasn't fair. My heart and body were teaming up against my head. I knew very well that falling into a relationship with the lycan meant trouble with a capital "T". Yet my heart wanted quite desperately for me to give him a chance, and my body agreed. The soulmark was also putting my hormones into overdrive. I had never felt so riled up by one man. Zoelle had been extremely flustered and confused at the almost ravenous state I described when in close vicinity with the lycan. Irina disgusted.

"Scoundrel," I mutter irately.

"Excuse me?" he asks, stepping forward, his towel slipping an inch.

"*Hmm?*"

"Did you say something?" he asks coyly.

Did I? "No," I say, fairly certain I hadn't. Or had I? His head cocks to the side, a hand running absentmindedly over his abs. "I, uh, I didn't say anything. You must be hearing things."

"Are you sure you didn't say 'scoundrel' a moment ago?" Shit. *Think, sober Sophie!*

"Keenan is actually out in the hallway," I tell him seriously. "I think you must have heard him. He was in *quite* the mood when I bumped into him."

"The scamp," he replies wickedly. "I always knew he had a thing for me." My mouth runs dry as I watch his fingers trail the swimmer's V he possesses. Almost teasingly.

I gasp in dismay.

"You're doing that on purpose!" I shout, pointing an accusing finger at him. "Put some clothes on," I hiss. "You *are* a scoundrel."

"I sleep naked," he tells me cheekily. Point Ryatt.

"Well," I sputter, still hypnotized by his languid movements, "you're not sleeping here." I can feel the weight of his gaze from across the room and fight the urge to throw myself at his feet. *Have some control*, I scold myself. *No mixing business with pleasure.*

"Is that what you really want?" I nod my head quickly. "Do you want to know what I want?"

My breath hitches at his baritone. I stop nodding, and my moment's hesitation is all that Ryatt needs to cross the distance between us. A blink of an eye and he is before me. His swiftness is unnerving, and I find myself laying a hand on his chest to stop the dizzying sensation that assaults me.

A warm presence falls to my waist as he steadies me. All the while those stormy eyes bore into me. With a gulp, I stare resolutely at his collarbone. I'm all too aware of how my breathing has turned irrationally erratic at our nearness. With a tug, I stumble into his body and feel his breath ghosting over my ear.

"I want you," he whispers, lips brushing against my ear. "And not just because of the soulmark, Quinn. And I think you want me too."

I jerk my head back to look up at him, eyes wide in confusion. "What?"

"You're an impressive woman, Quinn Montgomery. Entrepreneur. Clever. Witty. Beautiful. And quite the actress. What's not to like? I consider myself quite lucky to have you as my soulmark."

"*Oh.*" A sudden warmth flows through my veins, and I feel another stone being taken from my wall. I had not been prepared for this Ryatt. All charming and seductive. Silence falls thickly between us. My rapid heartbeat sounding like a heavy drum in my ear as I will my eyes to stay trained upon his collarbone. One look into his eyes and I was sure to be ruined. I try to think back on last night's encounter. The anger I felt, and how finding release on my own had been less than satisfying. But all I can seem to concentrate on is the scent of his shampoo. It's almost hypnotic, with its earthy undertones and hints of spice.

I should have bunked with Irina.

Ryatt slowly pulls back, his breath fanning across my cheek. The sensation curls my toes and kindles a fire inside me. I'm all too aware of the gentle throbbing of the soulmark against my nape. The effect that it seems to have over me when Ryatt is within reach. Though he might be certain of his feelings for

115

me, I wasn't so sure I could say the same for him. Not with my entire being at conflict. The soulmark only made my feelings more confusing, for I didn't know what was real and what wasn't. Or was it all real? I squeeze my eyes tightly shut, head swimming as I spiral suddenly downwards. The fire simmers to a halt.

"Where's your soulmark?" I murmur, shifting back and out of his hold. He releases me reluctantly, trying to catch my eye—something I resolutely ignore. Sensing the odd shift in my mood, he promptly lets his towel fall to the floor. "Ryatt!"

His laughter fills the air while my face burns brighter and brighter. "You can look."

"You're naked!"

"I am," he affirms. "I've also turned around. Do you want to see the mark or not?" I crack one eye open slowly, waiting for the hazy outline of his body to subside before zeroing in on his butt. A giggle bursts from my lips.

"It's on your butt?" I sputter.

Ryatt sends a wink over his shoulder, glancing down at his backside and giving it flex. Another giggle shoots forth. "Indeed, it seems it is."

I bite my lip to stifle the laughter that dares to burst forward. A sudden wish to have met Ryatt under different circumstances hits me hard. The smile on my face fades at the thought. As does super sober Sophie to be replaced with a much too vulnerable Quinn.

"You should go," I say and take a few more steps back.

He frowns back at me, "I know you have your doubts about all of this, but I should tell you that the wolf inside of me is all in Quinn. He's serious about you. He makes it so that all I can think about is you. About us. So I want you to know I'm willing to go all in too if you are. It's a risk, but it could be the best risk we ever take. Just think of how electric it could be. You and I together."

"Don't!" I beg, though my heart yearns to give in. To jump head first into all his promises and never look back. Luckily, all of my old heartaches rear their heads and squash the feelings away. "Just...don't. I want to sleep alone tonight, okay?" He seems torn, the frown on his face reading as frustration and disappointment.

"You can't keep pushing me away, Quinn. You can't keep playing all these different parts like it's some game," he says, dangerously soft. He picks up the towel and walks towards the bedroom door. "Your acts might fool the others, but I see you, Quinn. Little bits and pieces of the real you keep slipping through, and when you're finally ready to let her out I'll be here waiting." He departs with a sigh, the door closing behind him with a decisive snap.

CHAPTER 8
— Quinn —

There's nothing more annoying the morning after a night out than having to deal with someone who is annoyingly chipper. Ryatt and Atticus, who I learn is the Beta of the Adolphus Pack, send me and Zoelle cheerful smiles as they chat away like school girls. When Irina makes her entrance and sees our bleak faces, she turns back around and grumbles something about coffee to go. I cannot contain my look of envy.

"Buck up, darling. I'm sure Zoelle can cook up some hangover potion, can't you, soon-to-be-sister?" Zoelle gives a pathetic shrug but takes the bait and scampers off to the kitchen.

"Sweet dreams last night, Quinn?" Ryatt asks innocently.

"I slept fine," I inform him tartly.

"Ryatt told me you ladies got in fairly late last night," Atticus says brightly.

I spear him with a dry look. "I would never have

guessed."

"She's kinda cute when she's grumpy, man," Atticus says to Ryatt. The men clink coffee mugs.

"She is, isn't she. Her nose gets all scrunched up, and her lips do the most adorable pout. I can never take her too seriously," Ryatt responds.

"*She* is right here," I growl, "and she does not appreciate being talked about like I'm not." Atticus and Ryatt both chuckle. Atticus sends me a warm smile that has the irritating effect of softening my ire. He's a handsome man, in a very all-American kind of way.

"I want one," he says with a plaintive sigh.

Ryatt scoffs, "You have one, and come the new year she'll be here." I frown at the turn of conversation.

"What are you talking about?"

Atticus grins happily, "My soulmark was identified when I was eight, and she was five. Her name is Winter, and she's from one of the old Canadian packs. The packs knew we were both too young to do the full binding, and agreed that upon Winter's 25th birthday we could proceed."

"Oh," I try to inflect some enthusiasm into my voice, refilling my coffee. "That's good. Good for you Atticus."

"I'm pretty excited about it," he admits, completely oblivious to my forced enthusiasm. I smother a laugh with my fist. Excited was certainly one way to describe it. Thrilled, overly enthusiastic, and ecstatic would have also worked.

119

"I wouldn't be too excited about having the Blancs as in-laws," Ryatt informs me candidly.

Atticus flushes and shoots Ryatt a glare. "They're just a bit over protective of her. She's the last of the Blanc line, and I don't think they're too pleased that she'll be marrying a nobody like me."

Ryatt rolls his eyes, "All communication between the two of you has to be read and approved by her family first. That seems more than 'a bit over protective' to me. And do refrain from attempting to bad mouth yourself. You're the Beta of one of the fastest-growing packs in North America. One, I might add, that is growing stronger every day. You're a bona fide catch."

Atticus cracks a smile. "If I'm a bona fide catch, what are you?"

"A gift to the female race," Ryatt scoffs good-naturedly and sends me a wink. "*Obviously*."

"Is there a return policy I should be aware of?" I ask dryly.

"Have you finished your 30-day trial?" Atticus rebuts, crossing his arms over his chest. I give him a small grin.

"No, but—" Ryatt wears a satisfied smirk and shakes his head at me.

"Sorry, darling. Seems like you're stuck with me for another three weeks at least." I feel a small fluttering in my stomach at our relaxed banter and blame it on remnants of last night's drinking. Giving myself an internal shake, I hold back my retort and give them a strained smile instead. Sipping my coffee slowly, I sink back into my chair as the men continue the conversation between them.

My mind drifts. Treading softly over dangerous territory: Ryatt's promises. Old Quinn was trying to make some kind of comeback, and I was putting the blame on the soulmark, and Ryatt. His words had done a number on her heart and I could feel her presence lurking at every corner of my mind whispering at me to take a chance. That wasn't going to happen. All last night had ensured was that I needed to get a message out to my contacts and secure an exit plan. Ryatt would be lucky if I didn't find some way to leave once I had finished getting the crystal. The threat of going mad was somewhat more attractive when hungover, and my righteous anger from the other night finally found once more.

"Quinn?"

"Hmm?" I look sharply back at Atticus, who wears a charmingly small smile.

"Just wanted to say good luck today."

"Oh, thanks. You have a good day too." Atticus claps Ryatt on the shoulder as he stands, the action jolting him forward. His coffee spills across his emptied plate and Ryatt passes the Beta a scowl over his shoulder as he leaves.

"Shall we?" Ryatt asks.

"I'm sorry, what are we doing today exactly?"

"I've taken that pesky virus off your laptop. Today you can reach out to your contacts, and we can start planning how we'll tackle the artist premiere on Saturday. Remember, we only have five days."

121

I nod my head, closing my eyes as I set down my coffee and take a large breath. Just another job, and then I would find a way to move on. Figure out how to put a stopper on these feelings and just *go*. No looking back. Just like always. My eyes snap open, an easy smile on my face as I drown the feeling of anxiety that swells in my heart until it's only a distant murmur.

"Let's get this over with."

+++

We've taken up residence in a dark little room tucked away on the second floor filled with computer monitors and a number of fans. The sound of my clipped typing fills the silence between us. We don't speak as I work, but I am keenly aware of Ryatt's gaze. I try to slip in a couple of code phrases to Big Bear, my contact, as we communicate. Letting him know as discreetly as I can that I need my past deeds buried and to find me an exit after this job. One that would leave little trace of my existence.

"Okay, he should be sending me schematics of the loft sometime this evening. He was also able to track down an order for a jewelry safe from the company Brown Safe. It will have a key code pad, so I'll need an external EMF monitor or a black box. Those, and potentially something to dust the keyboard with, in case the latter doesn't work...wait, do vampires secrete oil?"

"I can get you the black box and dust by Wednesday," comes his soft reply. "And yes, they do.

You said he was slightly cool to the touch before. I take that to mean he has a heart stone ring. A vampire without is quite startling to the touch." I nod and take a large breath before continuing.

"Alright. Once we get the schematics, I'll need to reach out to a few other people to see if I can't secure the guest list to see who's catering."

"Mhmm," his hand reaches out to tuck an errant hair behind my ear.

"Are you paying attention to anything I'm saying?" I swat his hand away. Fighting the sharp urge to lean into his outstretched hand and find comfort in its warmth. Damn this soulmark and its plaguing hope and need.

The color of his eyes is like some kind of coming storm. A dramatic mix of pale and deep blues that lock me in place when I dare attempt to stare him down. "I've been paying more attention than you might give me credit for," he murmurs.

I swallow. *Keep it professional, Quinn.* "Do you have any questions?"

"I've copies of your history on at least two external hard drives. What good will come of you covering your tracks now?" Point to Ryatt, but at least he hadn't been able to understand my other coded messages. The ones to plan an exit strategy for myself.

"I don't want to make a habit of finding myself in this type of scenario again," I reply briskly, hackles raised.

"I doubt you'll be finding another soulmark," he counters. "There's only two to a set, after all."

"Yes, but who knows whose cock will be in my mouth next and proclaiming their undying love for me after?" Ryatt's jaw clenches at my blasé tone. "Or locking me in a kinky secret sex dungeon."

"You won't be leaving once the job is finished, Quinn. Surely you must have realized that by now. It won't be safe for you out there. Vrana will track you down faster than you can blink, and drain you dry. You'll stay here, in Branson Falls, and be safe. No one will be able to harm you once we have the crystals united and a protective border raised across our territory."

"And what, live here in domesticated bliss?" Tempting thoughts of a future with Ryatt strike at my heart. We would live together in some cabin. Deep in the woods. Surviving off an endless supply of champagne and fine foods as we indulge in each other's bodies. Again and again and again. *Damnit*. I cross my legs and stuff the image away. The only future ahead of me was comprised of me, myself, and I.

"You don't have to live here," he tells me, "but you won't be able to stay too far away without some discomfort. Not with the soulmark—"

"I'm sure I'll be fine."

"I don't think you quite understand the *profound* impact a soulmark has," he persists through gritted teeth.

"No," I respond in kind, blood beginning to boil. How could one man get under my skin so easily? "I do. Between that neat family dinner and girls' day

124

yesterday, I'm very knowledgeable on the subject now. I have half a soul; you have half a soul. They belong together, *blah blah blah*, eternal happiness, *blah blah blah*, or become sick with grief and madness. That about sums it up, right?"

"Don't forget the blinding pleasure of it all," he mentions, a chilling smile on his face.

I shrug. "Sorry, Ry-Ry, but it's already forgotten." My last comment seems to break the last vestiges of Ryatt's control. He darts forward, caging me in my seat with his arms. A devilish look on his face. My heart catches in my throat at the expression he wears as I steel my nerves for his retort.

+++

Ryatt

Who knew this little lamb would have such teeth? Maybe she was more wolf than she let on? The wolf liked the thought of that—very much.

It's a tiresome effort, but I manage to rein back the wolf as it prowls forward to the forefront of my mind. It has always laid a mite too close to the surface, but it had never bothered me much before. Yet ever since Quinn had entered my life—a flurry of golden curls, coy smiles, and designer shoes—it challenged my control every day. The wolf drove my possessive streak and my somewhat erratic and wild nature. At the moment the wolf didn't appreciate being reined back. It had gone from utterly smitten to crazy in love in a

125

matter of days. And it wanted me to take her. To lay the mark and bind her to me—to us. Though my infatuation remains, I can't deny the prospect of something *more* pleases something deep inside of me.

That's when I smell it. The sudden spike of her arousal.

I close my eyes with a growl and inhale the scent deeply. A triumphant smirk ensnaring my lips before I can help it. Perhaps the little lamb wasn't so afraid of the big bad wolf after all? We might dance around each other with carefully laid words and barbs, but a constant heat seemed to be simmering between us nowadays. Quinn could put on her many faces and personalities, but the nose didn't lie. She was attracted to me in Mexico before the soulmark, just as she was now. But it was more than the soulmark; it was us.

"No pithy retort?" Comes her breathless inquiry. I let my eyes slip open, knowing them to be shaded in gold. The sound of her heart gives off a shudder, her eyes dilating as she gazes up at me.

"Just one," I whisper before giving in and bringing her lips to mine. We meet with a groan. Tongues and teeth battling for dominance in a fight she cannot dare hope to win. Soon enough her lips fall into the rhythm of my direction. Sliding and caressing mine in the most enticing way. As I pull back her body follows, hands reaching out to pull me nearer. I can't help the smile that plucks at the corner of my lips. She must sense it for she pulls back with a gasp.

"You ass," she hisses, eyes blazing with heat. "You

disgust me." She stands abruptly and bolts for the door, but my hand catches her arm.

"I'd say your body tells a different story, darling," I tell her, standing as well. "There's something here between us. Like wildfire. You can't deny it. I feel it too."

Her gaze flickers uncertainly to me, and the wolf leaps at the opportunity. In mere seconds she is placed up against the wall, fans and old equipment dashed to the side. Our lips meet again, and her fingers dig into my hair. Desperate for a taste. Our hips shift. They push and grind until the pull to have her is almost too much to bear. The wolf howls its victory as I let out a shuddering groan. Then I tear myself away from her lips and drop to my knees.

+++

Quinn

He has my pair of Lucky jeans down to my ankles in three seconds flat. Pulls one leg free to hook over his shoulder and then drives his face between my thighs.

"*Jesus Christ*," I moan, bucking against the rough probing. My panties come away with two determined yanks, and I can barely think to scold him for the fever I succumb to. Why was I letting this happen? This was the very definition of unprofessional. And—*oh*—I couldn't possibly leave everything I knew behind for—*oh God*.

127

My sights set themselves upon the raven-haired man beneath me, and my mouth goes dry. There is something so right and oh so wrong about the sight that greets me. I feel as if I've surrendered to some out-of-body experience as I watch myself get tongue-fucked by this rakish devil.

Ryatt pauses to lick up the sides of my thighs and capture the slick heat which escapes his attentions. A finger probes my entrance, then another, his shining blue eyes locking onto mine just as he takes my clit in his mouth. I feel my straightened leg begin to buckle as he begins to suck in earnest.

"Ryatt," I gasp, hands reaching out to secure purchase around me only to witness a mountain of electronics tumble to the ground with my thrashing. My eyes turn towards the ceiling, even though they beg to watch the rest of the show. I curve into the air, back arching and pelvis inching forward as I lose myself to this inferno of pleasure.

A nip at my thigh drags me back to reality. Ryatt's hands find my hips and hold me steady until all I can focus on is the thrust of his tongue against me.

"*Oh God*," I whimper.

"Not exactly," he whispers, pulling away with a slick pop. His lips glisten from my arousal, and he marks a determined path upwards with his lip. Helping hands shove my shirt up and over my head as he raises to his feet. Mindless with the release I am denied once more, my hands reach for his belt.

"Quinn—"

There's a strange quality to his voice. An uneasy

plea I note as a warning, but that my hands do not heed. "Shut up," I breathe, smashing my lips against his. Hands lock around my wrists, halting my progress with his belt. "What?" I ask.

"I don't think you realize what you're doing," he tells me darkly, eyes almost completely golden. I shake off his grasp and grab hold of his length. Ryatt's eyes flutter close with a groan, body trembling with unsuppressed need. With a vicious growl, he kisses me. Our hands work in tandem to finish the job together. A stab of desire hitting me deeply. A sudden ravenous need surging through my body as I hook my leg over his hip. His cock at the entrance of—

"Fuck," I gasp against his lips at his entering thrust. Our eyes meet. The space between us contracting. "This is just mixing business with pleasure."

The words slip from my mouth before I can stop them, and Ryatt stills inside of me. "I'll show you pleasure you won't ever forget," he promises darkly before his hips bear down upon me. It draws another strangled cry from my lips as he begins a brutal pace. His hands move to cup my breasts. Roughly palming them through my bra and pinching at the hardened nipples. I whimper at his rough handling. Push my hips back against his to spur him on. There will be bruises. From both hands and lips. And I can't be bothered to care.

"And now I lay my mark for all to see," he whispers hotly in my ear, hips slamming into me with earnest. My hands claw at his shoulders for purchase,

REBECCA MAIN

his words like some distant memory in my mind. "By blood, be one."

A fleeting sensation of pain registers against my shoulder, as my orgasm shudders through me. It bends the back and curls the toes. Makes my moan sound loudly throughout the room. Ryatt's thrusts end in a havoc spasm, a terrible groan rumbling from his throat.

A nervous tremble steals over me as we untangle ourselves. Ryatt places a soft kiss against my forehead. "Business and pleasure," I mumble under my breath as I do up my pants, bitterness and sadness swelling inside my chest. I can feel Ryatt's disappointment without even looking at him.

"Something like that," he mutters in return.

CHAPTER 9

- Quinn -

It's Irina's look of mild revulsion and snarky comment some hours later that informs me of the significance of our...engagement. I'm a mixture of shame and fury and stalking the house to confront Ryatt. He's in the bedroom staring bleakly out the window.

"I'm sorry," he apologizes almost immediately, though he doesn't bother to turn around to face me. He must have heard my Manolo Blahnik sling-backs clicking and clacking throughout the house and my determined approach.

A surge of sadness and regret hit me in the stomach, the force of which almost sends me doubling over. Instead, the foreign feelings somehow dull the rougher edges of my own anger. I stand wordlessly in the doorway, at a loss for what to say. "What you said, that this was just mixing business and pleasure," Ryatt takes a deep breath, his hands forming tight

131

fists at his side. "It hurt. It hurt me, and I lashed out. I took advantage of the situation and let my wolf get the better of me. I'm sorry." He finally turns around then, his face contorted in the same agony as mine. "Who told you?" he asks.

"Irina. Something about finally smelling like 'Pack,' even if it meant smelling like you. Plus the bite mark on my neck. You broke the skin."

He swallows. "I was upset when I did it. I know I shouldn't have—"

"Of course, you shouldn't have. God! I am so angry at you right now." My body trembles with it and as Ryatt dares to take a step forward, I go one back. "Don't! Don't come near me, do you understand?"

"I'm sorry, Quinn. If I could take it back I would; I would have done it right."

"You wouldn't have done anything," I spit back, "because I wouldn't have agreed to completing another step of the soulmark!" His face pales. "After we finish with this heist, I'm gone. Fuck this stupid soulmark and your stupid pack of wolves. I make my own decisions from now on, nobody else."

His eyes fall shut as if he can't bear to look at me. I feel the same. There is such a torrent of emotion colliding through me it's almost as if I cannot breathe. Tears sting around the corners of my eyes.

"I'll make this right," he finally whispers. "I swear to you I'll make this right."

"Doubtful," I respond mournfully. Initiating the sex had been a grave mistake on my part, but Ryatt pressing on with the soulmark? How could I find it in my heart to forgive him?

An old hurt simmers inside me. This lack of control was frighteningly reminiscent of the one I faced in my youth when the most important decisions of my life had been made for me. With everyone thinking they were doing what was best for me. I leave without another word, the old hurt turning into a stone in my belly. With any luck, Big Bear and my other contacts would come through with my exit strategy. And then I'd be gone on the wind by the time our heist was through.

+++

There is no moving past my anger or the constant heartache that seems to plague me. Damn this soulmark and the way it twists my feelings. I have every right to be angry and upset, yet Ryatt's feelings shadow my every move. I'm wrapped up in feelings of guilt and remorse whenever I come too near, and when I see his crestfallen expression the nearly overwhelming urge to forgive him consumes me.

I give a small groan of frustration. That kept happening. Every time I seemed to be able to pinpoint my anger and move past the fog of Ryatt's emotions, my heart would give a tug and pull me back down into memories of his touch and his laughter. The marking hadn't just opened the link between us wider; it had also dredged up feelings for Ryatt I thought nonexistent. Begrudgingly I could admit that there was an attraction between us—chemistry even—

though I loathed to say it. I just hadn't realized that some part of me had enjoyed our connection more than I had been able to recognize. It seemed like a defeat after having spent so long keeping people at arm's length. Somehow he had wormed his way into my heart with that charming grin and vulgar wit.

But I couldn't forgive him. Monday went by in silence. I had kept myself neatly tucked away, hammering out the details of my feelings with red-rimmed eyes. Tuesday had passed much in the same fashion, with Ryatt stopping by once in the afternoon to try his hand at apologizing once more, a bouquet of roses and box of chocolates at the ready.

By the looks of him, he had been having about as good of a time sorting through our affairs as I had. Which is why on Wednesday, Zoelle took pity on me and drove me out to spend the day at her grandmother's.

"You two still aren't talking?" Zoelle asks as we drive along a tree-lined street.

"Definitely not," I respond.

Zoelle makes a right, her eyes swinging in my direction as we make the turn. "Xander did the same thing to me."

"He fucked you then abruptly left the room so you could stand around like some fool wondering what the hell just happened?" Zoelle colors.

"Not exactly," she hedges. I raise a dubious brow. "We were fooling around in my kitchen, and he seduced me. Kind of. I didn't even know until a week later that he had marked me. It was only because his mother accidentally let it slip. I was really confused as to why I was feeling so much more from Xander and why he seemed to have this unexplainable ability to call me to heel. Of course, I was equal parts furious and embarrassed, but it ended up being overshadowed by the death of his mom shortly after."

I stare at her in shock. "That sounds awful."

"I was in pretty bad shape," she admits sheepishly. "The current of emotion from the bond hadn't just widened between us. With the marking, you officially become part of the Pack, and I was feeling their loss too. God, it was such a cluster-fuck."

"Did you just curse?" Zoelle colors again.

"It's the best way I know how to describe the situation, okay?" she tells me defensively. "Anyway, I just wanted you to know I get it. That I understand how you feel."

"I don't even understand how I feel," I tell her with a sigh. She passes me a sympathetic glance.

"Pissed off. Uncertain. Upset. And maybe the tiniest ounce of hope?"

"Yes to the first three, and a hard no to the last. Why would I be hopeful?"

Zoelle chews on her bottom lip before answering, "Because despite everything, maybe deep down you like him."

"No," I tell her, staring out the window. "It's just the soulmark. It's not even real."

"The soulmark doesn't just make feelings appear. It amplifies what's already there in your heart. I'm going to take a wild guess and say you were attracted

135

to Ryatt when you first met him. He's a good-looking guy. Sometimes he's even known to be funny. Once the soulmark was sealed it probably latched onto that attraction and boosted it."

"Being attracted to someone doesn't mean you have to like them," I remind her.

"It doesn't," she agrees tentatively, "but you do like him, don't you?" I say nothing. "It's okay if you do. I was reluctant to admit my feelings for Xander when they started coming around. There was also the fact that I was also in another relationship at the time..." she trails off sheepishly.

"What happened with that?"

"I cheated on him," she whispers mournfully. "If there were anything I would have done differently, it would have been breaking up with Ben earlier. I put it off. I used him as an excuse to try and avoid my growing feelings for Xander. It ended pretty badly between us."

"You told your ex you cheated on him?" Zoelle nods. I let out a whistle, eyes widening. "You have some balls," I comment. "I don't think I would have had the nerve to do it." More likely than not, I would have dropped him cold without an explanation as to why. I had never been brave in matters of the heart.

"I barely did," she admits, "but Xander and I just had this moment of understanding. Of acceptance, really. I knew I couldn't leave Ben hanging like that anymore. What about you? Have you ever been in a similar situation?"

"Have I ever cheated on anyone? I guess I have. I

mean, I don't know for sure. I've never really been in a relationship before, but when the job calls for it, I play the role of girlfriend or mistress." I give a small shrug. "They never really meant anything to me."

"Did you have sex with them?" she asks, more than an edge of curiosity in her voice.

I give a little grin. "Sometimes," I tell her honestly. "I never had to if I didn't want to. But sometimes it was fun to mix business with a little bit of pleasure." A knot twists in my stomach at the phrase. Too bad mixing business with pleasure had led to such turmoil this time around.

"It probably feels even more confusing if feelings are there clouding the surface though, huh?" I nod slowly, swallowing the sudden lump in my throat.

"Is mind reading one of your witchy talents?" I comment lightly.

She shakes her head, pulling the car to a stop in front of a large house. "Like I said, I understand where you're coming from. I was in your shoes less than a year ago." She hops out of the car without another word, leading me silently into the house.

"Zoelle, is that you?" A woman calls out amidst a chorus of laughter down a short hallway.

"Yes!" Zoelle turns to me with a smile. "They're all harmless, I promise." She grabs my hand and drags me deeper into the household. My eyes dart wildly around, skimming the picture-lined walls and enjoying the scent of something sweet and chocolatey in the air.

I send a tentative smile to the women gathered in the room, all assembled around a small table near a large expanse of windows. Daylight shines in through the sheer curtains, casting them in a golden light.

"Come sit down," one woman says, the same one who called out before. I note the two empty seats and set of matching mugs set before them, steam billowing softly from both. A plate of cookies sits in the middle.

"I'm—"

"Quinn Montgomery," one of the other women supplies serenely. She has long white hair and pale skin that is scarred heavily in patches of pink and red. She smiles widely at me. "We know all about you."

"Quinn, meet Maureen Clybourn," Zoelle introduces us with a gentle smile. "This is my grandmother, Diana Baudelaire, and this is—"

"Lydia Stein." The last woman has her hair pulled back into a tight bun, her skin the color of cocoa. It's almost the same shade as Diana's. "How are you handling that boy?"

"It could be going better."

"She's being modest," Zoelle quickly quips. "She has him wrapped completely around her finger, and she doesn't even know it. Every other second he's making moon eyes at her, and they do this whole flirting-fighting thing."

"What?! We do *not*."

Zoelle gives me an innocent look. "Just because you're too blind to see it doesn't mean it's not happening." I must look like a fish out of water. I wasn't used to this sassier side of Zoelle.

"I'm not blind," I grumble. "I'm well aware of the fact that he's stalking me. And I'm almost positive I've seen him sniffing after me, like, literally sniffing."

"He's been pacing outside her door for the past day or two," Zoelle adds. The women look at me expectantly for an answer.

"He marked me," I tell them with a heavy sigh, "without my knowledge or permission."

"They were having sex—"

"Zoelle!" I shriek in outrage, "could you not divulge all the details of my life?"

"Sorry," she mumbles around her mug.

"He didn't pressure you into it, did he, dear? Sometimes the wolf inside them can grab control. They can be quite dangerous. If you need us to, we can put that dog in his place," Lydia states.

I shake my head. "It was most definitely consensual," I admit. *And completely my doing.* "We have a lot of...fire, between us. Plus, it's not the first time we've fooled around."

"Well, I don't know why you would go and have sex with the boy if your intentions weren't to complete the soulmark," Lydia adds. "Physical contact increases its effect and pull."

"What? It does?" I ask in a panic.

"Well, yes," she says, eyebrow cocked. "The soulmark desires to be complete. It is meant to be one, not two, and the physical contact drives this urge."

"I didn't know that," I tell them pitifully.

"Every bond is different to a certain extent," Diana tells me, reaching out to pat my hand. "Why don't you have a cookie, get some sugar in you. You're looking a bit pale." I snag a cookie and shove it into my mouth.

"Have you been eating enough?" I give a short nod and take another cookie. "Good. It won't do you any good to starve yourself." Her voice takes on a familiar motherly tone. The one you always hear in movies and TV shows.

"You've certainly gotten yourself into a jam," Maureen remarks, sipping on her tea. "Perhaps you should leave your life of crime behind for something more useful to society."

"It's what I'm good at," I tell her with a forced smile, "and it's what I like."

Lydia passes a speculative look at the two other women before pinning me with her stare. "You find fulfillment in stealing from others?"

"When you put it that way it doesn't sound very...nice."

"Well stealing isn't a very nice hobby," Lydia says with a snort, "and it doesn't seem to have done you any favors."

"It did put her in the path of her soulmark, Lydia."

She rolls her eyes. "It also had her steal from *us*, Mo. Or have you forgotten?"

"She'll get it back for us," Mo says solemnly, turning her intense gaze upon me. "Won't you?"

I finish my cookie and fight for some semblance of composure. It wasn't every day you had to confront the people you stole from. Not for me at least. "I have a plan. I'll get it back."

"Well, don't hold out on us dear. We want to know the details," Diana says, sitting back.

"Yes!" Lydia agrees eagerly. "I want to discuss

140

your plans with Kymberly Moon. If she has a clear idea of your plans, it helps her know what to search for in her premonitions."

"Her premonitions?"

The three older women nod their heads in unison. "She can see the future. It's come in handy more than once. I've been helping her learn how to focus her talents. If she can get an idea of any obstacles you might face, then you'll be one step ahead of the game."

"And you can get back that crystal," Maureen's endorsement is said with unusual gusto, and I give a small laugh.

"Okay, okay," I tell them with a small but honest smile. "I'm all for supernatural help." Or any help at all.

"You'll need all the help you can get if you're going up against a vampire," Diana says seriously.

I turn my sights on Zoelle, somewhat accusingly. "How much have you told them, exactly?"

"Just about everything," she admits sheepishly. "I couldn't not! You stole our crystal after all. They need to be kept in the know."

"And telling them about my private affairs with Ryatt fit how?"

Maureen lets out a sharp, bark-like laugh. "That man is a downright scoundrel, and his wolf is always near the surface of his mind. It makes him more impulsive. As if he's untamed."

"You think he's a liability?" I ask with a slight frown. "That the 'wolf part' of him will make him...I don't know. Do something to draw too much attention

141

to us?"

The women ponder my questions carefully. "I don't think so," Zoelle hedges carefully. "I think it will make him more overprotective of you, potentially even more careful."

"More paranoid," Lydia states coolly. "You'll need to stay calm. If he senses danger or anything that might endanger you, he'll react."

I nod my head thoughtfully. It was good information to know. I wasn't used to working with a partner on a job.

"I plan on getting in and out as quickly as possible. We'll have to mosey around for 20 minutes or so that I can show some face, but Mr. Vrana will most likely expect me to keep a low profile—so I will. The trickiest part will be getting to the safe without notice. It's in his bedroom on the second level. We'll take a staircase tucked away near the kitchen to go up, but the second-floor landing is in perfect view of the first floor."

"We can give you an aversion elixir," Diana tells me reassuringly. I give her a slightly bewildered look.

"I have someone on the inside stashing a pair of waiters' clothes for us to change into. They promised to make a small diversion for us, but we can take the aversion elixir too, for extra precaution. What does it do exactly?"

"Those around you will want to stay away from you and ignore you," Zoelle explains, "but only one of you should take it. I don't think the plan would go nearly as well if you suddenly don't want to work as a team any longer."

"The artist's work will be displayed throughout the place. I just don't know if it will be up on the second floor. If it is, we can slip into the bedroom more easily."

"And then?" Maureen asks.

"And then I break into the safe while Ryatt keeps guard. I double-strap the sucker to my thigh, and we get out."

"We'll get the elixir to Zoelle by Friday," Diana says, "and Mo will speak with Kym by then as well." A large smile splits across my face.

"Thank you. I promise this will go off without a hitch. You'll have your crystal back by Saturday night."

"Good," Lydia declares, "because our enemies are closing in, and by the looks of it, we're going to have another one added to the list once Saturday comes about."

CHAPTER 10
- Ryatt -

If there was one thing I was good at in life, it was fucking up. Fucking up my sister's attempt at a love life. Fucking up the retrieving of our allies' property. Fucking up my relationship with my soulmark. The robe Quinn has been using rests on a hook of the bathroom door. I snatch it and make my way over to my bed, flopping down upon it with a forlorn sigh. I bring the robe to my face and inhale. I also happened to be a master of being secretly pathetic. No doubt Xander would have been caught sneaking scents off Zoelle's clothing pre-binding. But not I.

The scent of Quinn lingers in the room, but it is strongest in the things she wears on a daily basis. The wolf takes to it like some kind of calming sedative and happily relaxes at the back of my mind with her scent surrounding us.

The wolf had reached a level of pathetic I hadn't known possible. It's not been two weeks and it's head over heels in love, while I'm left to try and keep our feelings separate. Mostly. Lust and love were two very different things, but with the way the wolf was projecting, I wasn't sure how much longer I could keep the divide up. I inhale deeply once more, enjoying the scent of jasmine and citrus and *Quinn*.

"What the fuck are you doing?"

I hesitate for a fraction of a second, my eyes flying open at the sound of her voice before I throw the robe down faster than humanly possible. "Nothing," I smoothly deny, sitting up and running a hand through my hair. "You're back."

She eyes me warily, shuffling from foot to foot. "Obviously," she finally scoffs, though I note it is half-hearted. I slowly get to my feet.

"And you're talking to me." She looks away uncomfortably. "I'm sorry, Quinn, about the other day. Truly. I didn't plan on that happening." She doesn't carry the same tense weight about her. Her shoulders are no longer hunched. Hands unclenched. Scowl...still mostly intact. Regardless, it's a welcome reprieve. Quinn remains silent. Gaze elsewhere. Mind whirling, no doubt. The wolf whines pathetically in the background of my mind, still distraught over her body language and reaction to the marking. It could not comprehend why she was so upset, but I did and was determined to give Quinn some distance. She deserved to make her own decisions, no matter how unpleasant the consequences may be for both of us.

"I'm still pissed at you," she finally says, eyes caught on the window. "And I'm still definitely not

145

okay with how any of this has played out, but…"

My breath catches as she swings her gaze my way. Her eyes are the most serene blue. Startling even from afar, if I could only be so lucky as to wash away the unease from them. I shove my hands in my pockets, dropping my regard to the floor submissively. The wolf had obviously been getting to me more than I realized.

"But I can't undo it. I can't change it, and I know that the marking probably wouldn't have happened if I didn't take your pants off," she flushes with remorse. "I talked with a lot of witches today and was pretty thoroughly shot down. Time-travel is a big no-no, apparently. Plus they put on a little magic show for me. So that's apparently a real thing. Witches."

"A productive chat then," I mutter under my breath. I chance a glance to see if she has heard my utterance but only a small scowl lines the features of her brow and lips.

"I'm not going to be in a relationship with you, Ryatt," she tells me seriously. "I'm not a relationship kind of girl. I don't do boyfriends. I barely do 'friends,' but since we are apparently stuck together that's what I can at least offer. Friendship."

I can feel my eyes narrowing in on her as the wolf prowls steadily at the front of my mind. *Mine*, it softly chants. As if I didn't know that already. "Friendship," I roll the word around on my tongue, not particularly liking the taste of it. "Why? I think we can both agree we're quite good at being much more. We haven't even explored all the things we might do—"

"Can we not go there?" She takes a deep breath,

her heart racing though she maintains a neutral facade. "I spoke with Zoelle—" I let out a dramatic groan "—and she said she was able to with Xander. I don't see why we shouldn't give it a try."

"One, their situation was completely different from ours. Zoelle had a significant other at the time, and my brother is a bully, as Alphas tend to be. Two, we've already had sex. I've felt you. I've been inside of you. That changes things—"

"No," she says sternly, "it changes nothing. We can put what's transpired between us in the past and move forward as *friends*. People can have sex and still just be friends. It's not impossible. Besides, it didn't mean anything."

"Like hell it didn't," I growl, the wolf echoing its displeasure with a snarl that almost bursts forth from my lips. "It was a fucking revelation. I marked you, and that means something. There's no more ignoring it. No more ignoring us." The wolf leaps to the forefront of my mind and I feel a streak of all-consuming possessiveness ram its way through me. Quinn swallows and stares me down determinedly. "Do you honestly believe we can be 'just friends' after all that's happened?" I ask, deliberately keeping my calm. I take a step towards her and watch silently as she fumbles back.

"I won't deny that whatever this fascination is between us will be difficult to ignore. In fact, the soulmark will make it more difficult, or so I've recently learned. Nevertheless, I think we can push past the awkwardness and find some kind of common ground—

147

without all the touching."

I mull over the words and find myself stuck on her comment about the soulmark. The soulmark didn't make things more difficult. What exactly was she talking about? "If by fascination you mean attraction, you're right. It will be most difficult to ignore. The soulmark," a satisfied smile takes up residence on my face as I recall some minor details regarding its influence, "amplifies feelings that are already there. You like me."

Her face flushes a telltale red, "It just means we already have a sort of rapport that isn't exclusively derived from animosity."

"You like me!" I crow, taking several steps forward. She peels out into the hallway; hands held up defensively as she glares at me from outside the door. "What are you doing?" I ask, watching in amusement as her skin shades an even brighter red.

"You're not entirely loathsome," Quinn bites out.

"Why are you out in the hallway?" I take a measured step forward and watch in befuddlement as she skirts backward. Again. "Why are you doing that?"

"I have to meet with your sister," she says feebly. But feeble is a very un-Quinn thing to be.

"You're lying." A spike of indignant anger flares through the bond from her end. "What aren't you telling me?"

Quinn hesitates, eyes darting around the room until they land back on the window, a long sigh drawing from her rosy lips. "Physical proximity increases the pull between us because we've already

engaged in rather...intimate positions."

I quirk a brow. "Are you referring to the fact that we've had sex, or was it the rather fantastic head you gave me? Or was it—"

"Yes. You ass," she huffs. Her indignation turns to anger. "I'd prefer if we maintained a certain distance from one another to put a stop to that."

I pull my hands from my pockets and cross them over my chest. The urge to move closer is almost irresistible with the wolf clawing and howling to drive me towards her. It's her scent that holds me back. A mixture of fear and resentment, along with a healthy dose of what can only be shame. *Space*, I remind myself and the wolf sharply, *she needed space.*

"I don't understand why you can't just give me a chance," I tell her softly. "There's something between us. Something not even you can deny, even with all your carefully chosen words."

"It's not that easy."

"It is," I insist, shuffling forward a few steps. Her eyes flutter close for a second as she warily shakes her head.

"It's not that easy, Ryatt. You're asking me to dump my old life completely in order to live with a pack of wolves. Literally."

"Would that really be so bad? No more stealing or putting yourself in compromising positions."

"I like my compromising positions, thank you very much."

"I'm sure I can think of a hundred compromising positions to put you in," I promise, not bothering to hide the hunger in my voice. Quinn takes two steps back, minutely shaking her head. I sigh. "Why don't you run along and find Irina? I've some work to do before the day's end."

She scampers away, her lips splitting into a cautious smile before leaving. In a few quick strides, I make it to the door and push it gently closed.

That was progress, right? Acknowledgement.

I would just have to find a way to capitalize on her confession before we completed the heist. Only time was not on my side. My feet steer me back towards the bed, and I pick up her robe once more, holding it against my nose. Her scent calms me and the wolf. Lulling it into a state of tranquility so that I can have some peace of mind and think without its commentary. I needed a plan. A way to prove my case with her. Show her that we could be so much more together than we could ever be apart. I grin as I inhale her scent once more. I had just the idea.

+++

Quinn

It had been a long day. Between the witches, Ryatt, and being roped into helping Irina plan some party, I barely had time to collect the rest of the information I needed from Big Bear and my other contacts. This shower was just what I needed.

The hot water shot straight between my shoulder blades, its persistent stream easing the tension away.

The nozzle was turned almost fully to the left, delivering an almost unbearable heat, but God did it feel good. My eyes open lazily to see that the steamy fog, once relegated to the shower stall, has ventured to envelop the entirety of the bathroom. To any other, the room might be mistaken for a sauna. My hands grope along the wall until they find the soap and loofah, then jasmine and orange blossom fill the air.

I can't remember the last time I have felt so relaxed. I make sure to drench the loofah in soap to achieve maximum lather before tracing it over my front. Across the shoulders and down my chest. Lower past my stomach to swirl around my navel, then a quick swipe down both legs, before repeating the process.

I'm not quite sure when the other set of hands comes into play, but they do not frighten me as I would have expected them to. My hair is smoothed over one shoulder, and lips press themselves against the nape of my neck. I gasp. A sudden passion and bliss engulf my senses before slipping away just as suddenly as it came.

"You've been in here for ages," Ryatt teases, lips barely skimming over the surface over my over-sensitized skin.

I let out a small hum of acknowledgment, taking a moment to catch my breath. "Women have more to do in the shower. I shampoo and condition. I shave."

"Lather, rinse, and repeat?"

"Exactly," I tell him with a Cheshire cat smile and lean back into him. He gently pries the loofah from my

151

grip.

"Well then, let me help you finish so that you can come back to bed." I receive a small nip of admonishment on my neck. His tongue darts outwards to catch the droplets at rest there.

The loofah drags down my spine, fingertips following in its wake. I let out a breathy sigh, back arching delicately as the loofah is dropped to the floor and hands take up the task. They spread the lather. Taking their time to give attention to every inch they meet. His fingers rubbing out the knots and kinks that lie between my shoulders. Ryatt's hands stop low on my waist, thumbs digging inwards in small circles.

"I'm glad you decided to give me a chance, Quinn," he whispers, nuzzling his head against mine with a pleased exhalation. "You won't regret it. I'll make every day a new adventure for us. Show you pleasures you've never experienced before."

My focus falters even as I slip deeper into his touch. Is that how my day had ended? I couldn't quite remember the exact conversation, but it explained why I no longer felt the heavy weight of indecision in my heart. One hand slips around to my stomach, fingers flaring to touch as much skin as possible. I shudder a sigh.

"But don't think I've forgotten about your punishment, Quinn," he purrs in my ear, pulling me back till I'm flush with his chest. The hand around my middle tightens minutely as the other trails to my ass. I feel my heart give a sudden lurch, nipples hardening in excitement and anticipation. "It seems you haven't either," he breathes harshly into my ear. A second later a sharp slap is delivered to my ass. I gasp at the stinging sensation, body flooding with need so strong I tremble.

Ryatt's breath skates over my soulmark in steady exhalations, which only drives my need further. His body shifts to the right, hand caressing the abused cheek before pulling back. My breath stalls. A crack resounds in the shower followed swiftly by my lust-filled cry. Once more his hand soothes the ache it creates, fingers slipping lower.

"Ryatt," I whimper, pushing back into his hand wantonly. He groans, his length digging into my side.

"As much as I would love to finish this," he tells me, lips coming to brush along my ear, "now is not the time or place, little lamb." He shushes me as I release a desperate whine, then he drops to a knee behind me.

The loofah is back in his possession, making slow circles across my calves, the heat of his breath fanning across my inner thighs. A short moan of appreciation slips past my guard as he pursues my thighs with the soapy sponge.

"What is it the time and place for?" I murmur, hand reaching out to the wall to steady myself. Once more he casts aside the loofah in favor of his hands, rubbing the soap into my heated flesh, the water making quick work of what suds stay behind.

"Love," he whispers, his voice taking on an almost faraway quality.

"Love?" I whisper back. The word strikes me with a painful jolt, bringing with it a startling dose of reality. I didn't recall any talks regarding love. Love was...love was out of the equation for me. I didn't need it. I didn't need...Ryatt's fingers dance along the apex of my thigh. Caressing and gliding over the slick flesh but never quite touching where it's needed.

"Stop thinking," he tells me, running his lips up and over my ass to the small of my back. "Just *feel.*"

Feel? Feel what? A strange nervousness settles in my stomach, the outskirts of my vision vibrating. Love? I gulp down the thick air. Why was it suddenly so difficult to breathe? My hands reach desperately along the wall to turn the shower off and end our encounter to find some clarity. They find nothing but cool tile. *That's not right*, I think.

"Quinn," Ryatt growls, suddenly in front of me, hands cupping my face. His blue eyes sucking me in effortlessly. There is a summer storm raging in their depths. "Just feel," he begs, tilting his forehead to rest against mine. The bond between us pulses with something almost otherworldly. It is warmth and sweetness, security and wicked promises all wrapped up in one.

"Please stop," I whimper, unused to such foreign feelings.

"Let me in. Let me love you." My head twists from side to side fretfully, tearing out of his mild hold. I wasn't meant for love. I wasn't good enough for love. My past had proven it to me over and over again. "Please." I stumble backward, feet slipping out from under me in my haste. There are no hands to catch me as I fall. The elusive pillars of steam slip through my hands until I—

—lurch upwards from my bed panting.

My eyes are wide and frightened as they dart across the dark bedroom. I can feel sweat beading on my forehead and the back of my neck along my hairline. My pajamas are soaked through. Dear God, what was that? And why had it felt so real? Still the bond pulses, even though Ryatt is rooms away. I whimper as the fragments of the dream slip from my grasp, leaving me only more confused. There would be no more sleeping for me tonight.

CHAPTER 11
- Quinn -

Friday is unbearable. I can barely look Ryatt in
the face as we go over the details of the heist with last
night's dream stuck in my thoughts. It had been so
real. So vivid. Part of me wondered if he had used
some kind of spell, but the notion struck me as being
more hysterical than logical. I might begrudgingly
admit to some supernatural force in the world, thanks
to the display Zoelle's "Coven" had demonstrated the
day before, but it hadn't washed away all my doubts.

Apparently, seeing *was* believing.

In the afternoon Maureen drops by with our
aversion elixir. She encourages us to use it wisely
while wearing the most peculiar frown. After a brief
hesitation she relays to us the two premonitions from
Kymberly Moon. One, that we would encounter more
than one foe on Saturday night. Two, that there would
be a casualty. Ryatt had gone into a fit close to rage,
demanding the whole thing be called off, which left me

only one choice: to go to his brother. I couldn't afford to miss my opportunity to slip away.

Xander had ordered with cool authority that it would continue as planned, though extra precautions would be taken as to the detailing of our security. Ryatt had stormed off after giving a strained affirmation of his Alpha's order. Even I felt pulled under by Ryatt's worry and anger, finding it hard to breathe for a scarce moment as Xander's heavy orders passed over to me as well. I whimpered my agreement, Irina catching me as my legs trembled beneath me. Ushering me to a chair, she proceeded to thoroughly shame her eldest brother for his heavy-handedness until Xander had muttered an apology. I wish she had done so for Ryatt, but I was informed he'd have a hard time listening to anyone but Xander or Atticus so close to the full moon.

That being the case, Xander followed begrudgingly after Ryatt while the Beta stayed with myself and Irina. His presence had an oddly calming effect, one I had noticed dimly before, but even more so now.

"All I want is a little bit of excitement in my life, but with Ryatt and Xander breathing down my neck I'll never have the chance. All I want is to date a little—what harm is there in that? But no! Not me, their *baby* sister. They're purposely cock-blocking me, Atticus!" Irina ends her rant with a dramatic sigh, throwing the best puppy-dog eyes I've ever seen Atticus's way. "You're the Beta. Can't you do something?"

"You want me to tell my Alpha how to treat his

sister?" Her shoulders slump in defeat, her pretty pout turning into a pretty scowl.

"What about Ryatt?"

Atticus looks at me pointedly, eyebrows shooting upwards. "The only way to run Ryatt off your trail is to put something else in his path."

"Hey!" I say, my handful of popcorn stopping halfway to my mouth.

Irina's eyes brighten once more. Switch flipped. Puppy-dog eyes activated and trained on me. "You have to distract him," she tells me primly, "with sex. It's been known to do the trick before."

"I am not having sex with your brother again," I respond back tersely, throwing my popcorn at her. "We're just friends now. Okay?"

She scoffs, "You don't actually believe that, do you?" She swats away the kernels in a flurry, directing her ire back on me once the task is complete. "You're already marked. You'll be bound soon enough. And! Every time you two are within five feet of each other I'm afraid I'll be privy to a porno," she snarks, nose scrunching in distaste.

"Not true!"

Zoelle walks into the room, her arms filled with grocery bags and a soft smile on her face. Atticus catches her eye immediately and shakes his head.

"Wait, don't go!" I call after her retreating form. "*Rude,*" I mutter beneath my breath.

"You're really not going to have sex with him?"

"Of course, I'm not," I tell her, flushing with embarrassment.

"But don't you want to be my sister?" I look to
Atticus for help. He offers me a kind smile then slips
the popcorn bowl out of my grasp, giving me a quick
shrug as his apology.

"You're wonderful, Irina, but I don't need to be
your sister in order to be your friend."

"But I need another sister so that both of my
brothers are fully preoccupied. I've barely even lived
as it is! I'm always under their watch or some other
wolf lackey."

"I take offense to that," Atticus chimes in via a
mouth full of half-chewed popcorn.

"I take offense to you never bothering to help me!"
Irina cries.

"I help," he says indignantly. "I've helped you
sneak out a few times. Remember?" Irina groans.

"Yes, but I was only a teenager then. I never even
got around to doing anything serious with a boy. And
now that I'm 'of age' as they so like to put it, I'll likely
never get the chance unless my soulmark pops out of
nowhere. With my luck, it will be on some ten-year-old
and by the time he's 'of age' I'll be a wrinkly spinster."

Atticus chews slowly. "You'd be in your thirties. I'd
hardly call that a wrinkly spinster."

"Useless," she bemoans, standing from her chair
dramatically. "The both of you."

"Well, that was interesting," I comment once I
believe her to be out of earshot.

"It loses its interest after the sixth or seventh
time," Atticus tells me dryly. "But I get why she's
frustrated. They do keep her on a pretty tight leash,

and she just wants to have fun before she finds her soulmark. *If* she finds her soulmark. She also doesn't want to be a virgin anymore," he tells me with a quirk of his lips, "but no wolf from the pack is brave enough to face the wrath of her brothers, and she's too watched to make off with some random human."

"Holy shit, she's a virgin?" I whisper, aghast. "No way. Irina is a straight-up 10. Sure, her attitude is a bit bratty sometimes, but she also wears her heart on her sleeve. I can't believe she's never had sex. I'd probably have an attitude if I weren't getting laid on the regular too." Atticus snorts as I nod my head knowingly. "What? Maintaining a healthy and somewhat regular sex life is good for a person. It gives you happy endorphins, it's fun, and it can also be a real workout. If you know what I mean." I tick off my logic on my fingers, then wiggle my eyebrows for Atticus, though not very well.

He lets out a boisterous laugh, "Aw man, you're pretty funny."

"I know," I chirp, entirely too pleased with myself.

"You know you're perfect for him right?"

My pleasure vanishes with a groan. "Not you too, Atticus. I was just beginning to think being a prisoner here wasn't so bad with you here to keep me company."

He munches on a handful of popcorn thoughtfully, eyes scrutinizing me. "Do you honestly believe you're a prisoner here? That he would force you to stay if you didn't want to? You could have gone to the Baudelaires'. You could have tried to make off during your little shopping trip with Irina and Zoelle. You're the one who decides to keep yourself locked up in that bedroom all day."

"Yeah, so that I don't have to run into Ryatt and deal with his—his weird wooing attempts."

"Or because you're scared of him."

"I'm not scared of him!"

He shoots me a disapproving glare. "You're afraid of what you could have with him. Security. Love. A family. All the things you probably didn't have when you were growing up, if Ryatt's information was correct."

I feel my face flush unbearably red, and traitorous tears begin to swim in the corner of my vision. Point to Atticus. There seemed to be no running away from my past with this group of wolves. It was becoming far much more than an annoyance. Would I ever have the upper hand with them?

I take in a couple of deep breaths, willing my emotions away. Atticus lets out a small whine, moving to the seat next to me before I can find my feet and leave. His large hand takes mine. "You don't have to be afraid, Quinn. Change is scary, but taking that leap of faith is worth it."

"I really don't want to have this conversation, Atticus," I tell him tightly, hating the way my throat felt so constricted. I make a quick swipe at my eyes, dashing away any evidence of my heartache.

"I'm the Beta, Quinn. Most of my responsibility falls to making sure my wolves and their soulmarks are happy and safe. To make sure they know they are loved and taken care of. You can confide in me."

I swallow past the lump in my throat. "I think I'll head to bed." I avoid his knowing gaze and tug my hand from him. I didn't need any more lectures or opinions on how I should handle the soulmark. I knew exactly what I was going to do, and with the help of a few friends, I'd put my plan into action after the heist. "Big day tomorrow and all," I explain with a brittle smile, then walk out of the room without another word.

+++

"This is it," I tell Ryatt, pointing to the hotel on the right. He pulls up without comment to the valet stand, exiting the car to open my door while tossing the keys to the valet. "Thank you." Ryatt makes no comment, which shouldn't surprise me, as he's barely said one word to me the entire day. Since Denver was over a 10-hour drive, a private jet was procured to cut our time. Doing so also meant we now had a much stricter timeline to adhere to in order to take the jet back to Montana. Well, at least Ryatt did. If M pulled through on her promise, I'd find myself with my own transportation out of the city.

I slip my hand into his preferred arm, and he guides me inside the hotel lobby. "Your Mr. Vrana lives in a hotel?" he asks quietly as I hand over the invitation to the security guard waiting at the private elevator.

"The top floors are all condominiums," I explain,

taking back the invitation without a smile from the security guard. My eyes take a quick skim of the names checked off on the clipboard he holds. It seemed that just over half had arrived. Good. With more people trickling in after us our host would be preoccupied. "You should have worn the navy blue," I continue as we enter the elevator, feeling my ire tinge my words. "You'll draw too much attention in that color." That color being an *electric* blue. He would certainly draw every eye in the room.

"It's an artist premiere. I'm sure there will be guests dressed far more extravagantly than you or I," he responds quickly.

"Listen," I begin, feeling rushed as the numbers continue to tick up past the teens. "I need the suave and charming Ryatt, not paranoid, moody Ryatt. As far as everyone knows we're just another pair of guests set to enjoy the night."

He stiffens momentarily, eyes catching mine in the mirror as I touch up my lipstick. "I'm not moody or paranoid," he quietly seethes, "and if I was, I'd have every right to be. We're walking in knowing one of us isn't going to come out."

"We don't know that. It could be anyone in there."

"*You* don't know that," he whines, eyes squeezing shut as if in pain. "The thought that I might lose you just when I've found you." My breath catches, our eyes meeting once more in the elevator mirror.

"We'll be fine," I reassure him, gently squeezing his forearm.

"And what of the other enemies?" he asks, the

163

elevator beginning to slow as it nears the penthouse suite.

"Just eat them. Or something. You're a wolf, for God's sake. Growl viciously, I don't know."

The sparkle of amusement returns to his eyes as the elevator dings and the doors open. My heart skips a beat, realizing I had missed seeing it over the past few days. "I think we both know I'd rather dine on you," he purrs into my ear as he guides us out. A few people look our way, their curiosity mollified to see just another young couple. We make our way to the bar, slipping through the crowd with matching smiles. Ryatt nods to a fair few who eye us up, while I give a delicate wave of my fingers. No one approaches, our steps clearly intent.

"Dirty martini," I tell the bartender off-handedly, turning back around to face the crowd.

"Make that two," Ryatt corrects smoothly, keeping his back to the masses and scanning the people crowding around some art piece at the far end of the room. My eyes catch the familiar figure of Mr. Vrana. As if sensing my gaze, his eyes find me. Fresh martini glass in hand, I lift it in his direction. I'm aware of Ryatt tensing ever so slightly by my side and give a salacious wink and grin towards my employer before turning around with a swing of my hips and gluing myself to Ryatt's side. His hand finds its place low on my hip, and he presses a kiss to my cheek.

Our eyes catch as he pulls away, a familiar, knowing grin on his face. "If you don't calm that heart of yours everyone will hear it," he teases, but I know a warning when I hear one. "It seems like the artist has set up displays all over the condo. There's one outside on the deck," he points to the glass wall to our left that overlooks a massive outdoor patio, "one in the back. A few scattered about the main floor, and one or two on the second."

"What are we waiting for then?"

We make quick work of the first floor, stopping briefly at each art piece. Letting our faces be seen for only a short amount of time and doing our best to be unnoticeable. Ryatt was right. Tonight, the crowds gathered to impress with their haute couture outfits. Women in daring plunges and spiked shoulder pads. Men in bold shades of red and green.

"I've been told there is a restroom I might use upstairs," he tells me as we pull away from an arrangement of fragmented crystals stacked precariously together under a blue light. My eyes glance at the clock on the wall. It's almost 11:30 p.m. My contact on the inside was going to create a small diversion at 11:40 p.m., giving us roughly ten minutes to crack into the safe, steal the crystal, and make our exit. Any more time away from the party could potentially draw unnecessary attention.

"Alright, don't leave me waiting too long or I might just have to join you," I recite over the rim of my coupe glass. The air between us grows thick with heat. The hair on the back of my neck rises as he places a languid kiss on my shoulder. Teeth and tongue graze the skin as he pulls back to make his way inside.

"I don't remember allotting you a plus one," a cool

voice says behind me. My heart skips a beat as I turn,
a coy smile on my lips.

"You'll have to take it up with your secretary," I
retort.

"Are you enjoying yourself?" Mr. Vrana asks,
taking my free hand and dropping a kiss to my
knuckles. I fight the shiver that begs to race down my
spine at the cool pressure.

"It's not exactly to my taste," I admit, taking a
modest sip from my martini. "I like my art romantic
and dramatic. Not questionable craft projects."

Mr. Vrana laughs, a deep vibrato that draws
stares from the women and men crowded outside. "I'm
well aware that such modern art isn't to everyone's
taste, but I generally find the inspiration behind them
quite fascinating." His relaxed disposition keeps my
pulse steady, though for a brief moment I am lost in
his eyes. The pale blue is streaked with what looks
like mercury, something I am now much too keenly
aware marks his vampirism. "Don't enjoy yourself too
much, Ms. Montgomery," he murmurs, aware of the
effect his mesmerizing gaze has on the opposite sex.

I conjure a meek grin. "Of course." He departs with
a pleased smile, wandering to meet another group
sitting around the electric fireplace. I down the rest of
my martini and place it on the tray of a passing
waiter, making my way inside with my head held
high. No one pays mind as I make my way upstairs,
and so I weave about the people unnoticed. Several
have herded themselves around what looks like a trio
of pieces, dotted along the second-floor railing. A

perfect cover, yet even some from this crowd would find it odd if I slipped silently into one of the rooms.

My hand dips into my purse and grabs my phone. I press it to my ear, plaster on a brilliant smile, and begin to chat with no one. Feigning a need for quiet, I knock surreptitiously on the door I know to be the master bedroom. Cradling the phone between my shoulder and ear, I slip inside. A sudden squeal of excitement sounds from downstairs just in time for me to shut the door. I couldn't have asked for better timing.

"What took you so long?" Ryatt demands, nearly pouncing on me as I lock the door behind me.

"Mr. Vrana wanted to have a quick chat. I thought I could allow him as much seeing as how I'm about to double-cross him," I quip, and walk to the master closet.

Ryatt's hand falls heavily on my shoulder, spinning me around and crashing his lips down onto mine. I moan into the kiss. Feel that familiar electricity race between us. The kiss is filled with desperation. A perfectly controlled chaos, even as he pulls away with an almost painful whine pulling past his throat.

"I thought..." I shiver at the uncertainty I hear, can feel myself shifting into his embrace. How was I supposed to leave him when he kept leaving me so utterly breathless with his sincerity? Playful and mildly vulgar Ryatt I could deal with, but it was becoming remarkably clear that serious and thoughtful Ryatt was the more dangerous of the two.

I keep my eyes closed, and place a hand over his. The one that remains cradling my face. "I'm fine. Everything is going according to plan, but we are running low on time. Stay near the door and listen for anyone who gets too close, alright?" He steals another kiss, then does as I say, eyes trained on me as I make my way to the back of the closet. He's moved the dresser that hides the safe and placed the decoy at its foot for me. How sweet. Digging into my purse, I lay out the black box, fine white powder, and fingerprint brush.

The black box adheres to the front of the safe using a magnetic charge. I press two buttons in quick succession; the first turns it on, the second activates the electronic transponder. While the black box is busy figuring out the combination, I prepare the powder and brush. If it failed, I would have to go old school.

"Time?" I call softly.

"11:37." Plenty of time. The little red light on the black box flashes, signaling that it's finished. "Are you almost done?"

I roll my eyes, my fingers quickly typing in 8-7-2-6-2, then hit the green confirmation button. The locks pull back with a satisfying and distinct thunk. I open the safe and quickly scan the contents. Envelopes, a few stacks of money, some jewelry cases. None big enough to hold the crystal. My eyes focus on the lockable drawer, and I let out an exasperated sigh, snagging the small lock pick essentials I always keep on hand.

"11:38," Ryatt calls.

168

"I don't need a minute by minute update," I say
under my breath while fishing out a tension wrench
and pick. The next part is nearly as easy as the first,
but that's only because I've done this so many times
before. I insert the wrench into the plug, twisting it
carefully to the left before inserting the pick and going
about lifting each pin.

"11:39."

"Would you shut up," I hiss.

The lock rotates under some light coercion, and the
drawer opens. The crystal lies in a soft foam bed,
unchanged from when I first saw it. I let out a brief
sigh of relief, then get to work double-strapping the
crystal to my thigh. I move with methodical intensity
once I've placed the decoy. Close the drawer. Re-lock
it. Close the safe and set the alarm.

"Let's go," Ryatt calls just as I'm finished.

"The dresser, you idiot." He hustles over, ushering
me away. "I'll meet you downstairs."

I don't bother to wait for his response, pulling out
my phone once more and holding it to my ear. "I'll talk
to you later, darling," I coo against the mouth-piece,
closing the door softly behind me as I fumble to put
my phone back in my purse. Only one woman bothers
to spare me a glance, but her attention is soon
returned to her conversation. I make my way
purposefully downstairs. I couldn't afford to stop; the
crystal would be too noticeable.

A quick glance over my shoulder and I spot Ryatt
leaning against the banister, thoughtfully surveying
the crowd. Our eyes meet and we exchange matching

smirks. All we needed to do was make it to the elevator without incident. And then we would go our separate ways. I swallow down the pang of guilt it brings me, sneaking one last look up at the beautiful man. He watches me rather intently, sending a very well-timed wink my way to break me out of my reverie and make me bump into someone.

"Excuse you," the woman snarls. My apology halts halfway across my lips at her superior tone. I take a short step back, eyes darting across her figure as I make a succinct evaluation of her person. An Oscar de la Renta 2014 Spring Collection sporting a brocade of flowers over a light grey pinstripe dress. I roll my eyes, hardly impressed with her choice of attire and attitude.

"Have a nice night," I simper, blowing a saccharine kiss as I continue on my way. Her blue eyes shine with vengeance at my snub, but then she's flipping her brown curls over her shoulder and strutting away.

A clatter sounds outside, the product of a series of glasses and plates crashing into the ground. All eyes turn to the patio. Mine skirt to a clock on the wall which reads 11:41 p.m. *Better late than never*, I think as I eye the redhead outside along with the others. She stares aghast at her misfortune, her tearful gaze swinging around fretfully. Her eyes linger on mine a second longer than necessary, and I pick up my pace, a shot of anxiety bolting through me. The diversion would only hold people's attention for so long, and we needed to get out ASAP.

A hand falls to my lower back, urging me forward,

and then Ryatt is at my side. Another bout of dread fills my blood and I dare not say a word as I attempt to keep my heartbeat under control.

"Everything alright?" I ask casually as we enter the elevator. His hand carries a nervous tremor, but Ryatt's face is the picture of neutrality as he stares out into the pool of guests who have resumed their conversations. Ryatt presses the lobby button impatiently while I smooth my dress. I take a deep breath, forcing myself to relax. Everything was going to be fine, but for whatever reason, I didn't think I'd be heading off on my own tonight. *Damn it all.*

The elevator dings, the doors finally beginning to close, when I see Mr. Vrana approach the surly brunette. There's something strange about the way they greet each other so...formally, and then the brunette's icy blue eyes swing to us, followed by Mr. Vrana's. Ryatt barely contains his growl, the doors shutting just as I see the vague visage of rage flash over Mr. Vrana's face.

"Ryatt—"

"We need to get back immediately," Ryatt says, pulling out his phone and typing a furious message, which fails to send in the steel box. "We've been made," he says crossly.

"How? I don't understand."

He groans, running a hand over his face and beginning to pace the elevator. "That woman was Carrie Wselfwulf, the new Alpha of the Wselfwulf Pack."

I pale in understanding, "They're the ones who

171

want to attack your pack, aren't they?" He nods curtly.

"There's only one reason she would be there," he continues. "To negotiate for the crystal."

"You think they're working together?" I ask uneasily.

He shakes his head, resuming his place at my side and unbuttoning his suit coat as the elevator slows to a standstill.

"Not likely, but she must have had something that he wanted enough to trade for the crystal."

"What?" I ask as we rush to the valet.

"I don't know," he mutters, casting me a sidelong glance, "but we're going to find out."

CHAPTER 12

- *Ryatt* -

I have a hard time meeting Quinn's gaze and inquiries as we journey home, so the last few hours' ride from the airport to Branson Falls is filled with tense silence. It doesn't make matters much better that I have tampered with our soulmark bond, lessening the flow of emotions between us so as not to clue her in on my fears.

Quinn holds the crystal delicately in her lap, sights set upon something far off in the distance until she drifts off. The gentle stir of her breathing and her nearness soothe my jarred nerves. Xander would be expecting us, but first and foremost, the crystal would need to be delivered to the Trinity Coven's base at the Baudelaire household. I do not bother to wake her when I pull up to the house; instead, I slip the crystal from her lax hold and exit the car as quietly as possible.

"You two stay out here and watch her," I command

as soon as the other car arrives with our backup.
Joshua and Jordan linger at the car while Wesley and
Keenan trail after me.

The house is only somewhat familiar to me, having
only been here a time or two with Zoelle, but the thick
coating of magic in the air had left both me and the
wolf uncomfortable. Being deep within the coven's
territory would make any wolf feel on edge, and it
hadn't changed much since becoming allies. All that
magic snared the senses and left a wolf
feeling... *vulnerable*. How Xander had managed to
come here so many times was beyond me.

"Honey, I'm home." My lighthearted tone garners
various reactions with my accompanying grin that
shows a tad too much tooth. The wolf's hackles raise
as it counts the witches in the room: 3, 7, 16...it might
as well have been the entirety of the coven. "Am I late
for the party?"

I uncover the crystal from behind my back with a
flourish and place it on the table. There is a collective
sigh of relief echoed throughout the room, and Zoelle's
grandmother comes forward.

"Maureen?"

"I'm already on it," the other woman replies,
bangles clinking together as she takes the crystal. Her
hands, scarred from the battle those odd months ago,
take hold of the crystal reverently. She chants
something otherworldly under her breath and the
room comes to a stall.

The air tightens with a palpable tension. One that
pulls taut at the skin. I force myself to remain at ease,

but my companions seem unable to hold the same composure. Through the pack bonds I feel their tense anticipation and unease as a strange orange glow begins to emit from the palms of the old woman's hands. The crystal does nothing at first, and then with a sudden *crack*, it emits an almost blinding light. I flinch back, eyes warily trained on the mystical crystal as Maureen steps back.

"It's the other half," she tells Diana, face drained of color but beaming with delight.

"Ryatt, thank you," Diana says, reaching out and shaking my hand. I let my grin drop down a notch into something less wild and incline my head.

"Think nothing of it. I lost it in the first place. It seems only fitting I should be the one to fetch it back."

She raises a knowing brow. "As I recall, you were also the one to locate the other half of the crystal originally. You don't give yourself enough credit."

My grin quirks back up. "Too right you are, Diana. Let's call it a wash, shall we?" She pats the back of my hand and goes back to her chair, sitting in it with a sigh.

"We'll join the crystals tomorrow as soon as the full moon is in plain sight," Diana tells the room. "Be mindful of your schedules. I want everyone showing up to their shift at the border on time. No excuses. We cannot afford another month to pass."

A young woman raises her hand from the back of the room. "Can we cut back the rotation shift to three hours instead of four? By the last hour I'm completely drained, and I can barely keep my share of the protection spell up."

"Tracy Qualta, if you practiced and studied your magic nearly as much as you strutted around town looking for boys, you wouldn't find yourself so 'drained.'" Lydia Stein leaves no room for further argument with the look she sends the girl. "If anyone else feels too drained to protect this coven, I advise you to beg mentorship from the witches pulling six-hour shifts and acting as anchors. You don't see them complaining." A number of women shuffle uneasily and shoot guilty glances amongst themselves.

"I do love a woman in charge," I confess. Leaning against the kitchen island, I send a wink the older woman's way, enjoying entirely too much the way her lips twitch to hold onto her stern facade.

"Speaking of women," Diana says lightly, "How is yours faring?"

The wolf perks at the mention of its intended. As do I. "She's resting in the car."

"And Moon's premonitions? What of them?"

"She's one for two, it would seem," I inform her tightly. "We encountered the Wselfwulf Alpha upon our departure. It was quite unfortunate timing. There's no doubt in my mind; they'll attack tomorrow, if not tonight. They're well aware of the significance of the crystal and the power to be wrought from it. They were there to secure it from the vampire, though what they could have offered in return to entice him I'm not sure."

The Elder Triad share a meaningful look before Diana sighs, "We might have some idea as to what the vampire might want. Though I doubt the Wselfwulf Pack has it."

"Do explain," I reply softly. Diana straightens.

"The Amethyst of the Aztecs."

"I thought all that remained of the amethyst was divided among the higher echelon of the vampire families? No new amethyst has been found for hundreds of years," I tell them patiently. "I can certainly understand why a vampire would want one, but why would he think the Wselfwulfs could deliver? If that is what they had in mind to trade."

"In order to secure the Crystal of Dan Furth originally, we made a deal with the Stormrow Clan. In exchange for the crystal we would supply them with the amethyst, set in the traditional golden ring." She pauses, letting her eyes narrow upon the scowling faces behind me. "The exchange, of course, did not go as planned." Diana waves a hand towards Maureen and her scarred skin. "We received only half of what we were promised, and the Stormrows received a forgery."

"A damn good forgery," Lydia mutters.

"Does my brother know of these details?" I ask quietly, staring intently at Diana and homing in on her heartbeat alone. If she were to lie, I would be able to tell.

"No," she says stiffly, "only that the trade went awry and half the crystal was missing."

I let out a controlled breath, "How very interesting. Did you ever have the original to begin with? Is it somewhere safely hidden?"

"We never had it in the first place," she tells me. There is no tick in her composure. No jump in her pulse. No tell at all that she is lying. "We learned through our sources that the Stormrows were poking around for something of the sort, and knew they had the crystal in their possession. It was obvious what we had to do."

"Why were they inquiring about it in the first place?"

Hackles raised, Diana glares at me blandly. "It was obviously for that vampire. If he wants the ring desperately enough to seek aid from sorcerers and make deals with savage wolf packs, then I'd suggest we find the ring first. No good can come from a single more of their kind being able to walk in the light among us."

"I'll be sure to inform my brother of your suggestion," I tell her. Several thoughts begin to brew at the back of my mind. "I don't suppose your seer might be able to point us in the right direction of where to start sniffing? If not, Keenan will be more than adequate in helping me search out the ring. After all, he was a considerable help in finding the crystal in the first place."

I send a cool glance over my shoulder at the burly man; tattoos scour his body almost as thoroughly as the scars covering Maureen. He's certainly not a man to be trifled with, but once his loyalty has been gained, there is no better man to have at your side. He gives the slightest of nods at my acknowledgment, ever the humble giant. I roll my eyes back towards the witches.

"He's proved himself an asset to our mutual cause, so please ask your seer to keep us in her thoughts, or whatever it is she needs to do to gain her foresight. I'm not quite certain I understand the framework or basis of summoning such premonitions. Perhaps some time we can discuss it?"

"Not likely," a voice replies sternly from the crowds. I perk up, eyes searching for the witch. She's quite small, just over 5 foot 2 inches, but by the looks of her clothes, which don't seem to fit, she's got more growing to do. It's understandable considering she's still only a teenager. Her brown eyes drill into mine, and even from afar they are sparked with righteous anger that I'm sure I don't deserve. A sharp pang of grief hits me through the soulmark, followed by a wave of grief. I turn my gaze towards the entrance hall instinctively.

"Well, well, the little kitten has claws, does she? I thought you'd be taller, Moon." My gaze flickers back to her like an afterthought, and she takes a menacing step forward. "You might try working with her a bit more, Diana. We'll need more consistency in her premonitions if we want a chance at finding the ring before the Wselfwulf Pack or the vampire."

The front door opens and closes faintly, but the sound of multiple people shuffling through the hallway is loud enough that the room awaits the newcomers. Quinn comes in, face eerily white with Jordan and Joshua crowding behind her.

"What's wrong?" I ask, instantly coming to her side.

I take a deep breath and am flooded by the scent of her anguish. I struggle to open the bond back up, but once I do am pummeled by the onslaught of her emotions. Quinn comes willingly into my arms, dropping her head against my chest as she takes deep, steadying breaths. "Tell me," I demand, arms tightening around her. "What's happened?"

She pulls back long enough to pass me her phone, a picture already pre-loaded onto the screen. My eyes take in every detail. A beautiful woman lying prone on the ground, her red hair stained darker by the blood spilled savagely from her throat.

I take a deep breath and find my forced composure once more. "Who is this?" I ask quietly, turning off the screen and pocketing the phone. There was no need for her to continue staring at whomever this acquaintance was. I should have never returned her phone.

"It was M," she whispers mournfully. "She helped us tonight. She—"

"Provided the distraction?" She nods her head and takes several shaky breaths, dashing her tears aside determinedly.

"Yes."

"I see," I murmur, turning my hooded eyes Moon's way. She shrinks back in response. "I suppose your premonitions were right after all."

"There's a lot to do before tonight," Diana says sagely. "I think it best you all head home and get some sleep."

I give Diana a curt nod. "We'll be in touch." I steer Quinn out of the room swiftly, blood racing at the new information. Mr. Vrana's retaliation had been swifter than I imagined. Diana was right; finding the ring first was paramount.

We arrive back home in no time at all. There's hardly any traffic to worry about so early on a Sunday morning. Not in this perfect suburbia nestled in the woods. Quinn is unnervingly quiet during the last stretch, her composure giving barely anything away. Yet I can feel her torment and guilt tearing through her, courtesy of the bond. It drives the wolf nearly mad when I let go of her hand to keep both of mine on the steering wheel, but I won't let it blindside me.

"You're back!" Zoelle stops midway up the master staircase to watch us file in, her eyes both excited and wary at the sight of us. "You delivered the crystal?"

"Yes," I reply. "Where's Xander?"

She hesitates, acting as if to come down and greet us, but when her eyes stay glued on Quinn a touch too long, I let out a small growl of warning. Zoelle's eyes shoot straight to mine, a flush drawn up upon her skin. "I'll go get him. Go to the study and I'll tell him to meet you there."

Keenan lingers with Wesley in the background waiting further instruction, but with a short wave of my hand I dismiss them.

"Go take a shower and rest. I'll meet you in a bit," I instruct Quinn softly as we make our way upstairs. My hand itches to rest upon her hip. To provide some means of comfort, even in such a small gesture, but I refrain. I follow a few steps behind, turning in the opposite direction once we've reached the top and head

181

to the study.

The wolf grumbles its displeasure in my head, but I corral it to the back of my mind, tempering it with the knowledge that we'll only be apart a few minutes more.

"It's a bit early to be drinking, even for you," Xander informs me once he enters, displeasure neatly hedged in his voice. I shoot back my small pour of bourbon with a grimace, then send him a rueful grin.

"It's never too early to celebrate, brother," I retort, pouring another shot into the crystal tumbler. "The crystal has been returned, and we've all returned unscathed. For the most part."

"Zoelle said Quinn seemed *off*, and I can feel her sadness through the pack bonds. What happened?"

The next shot goes back much easier. "One of her acquaintances was killed tonight for helping us. A picture of proof sent courtesy of our dear Mr. Vrana."

"You didn't mention this when we spoke earlier."

"It only just happened," I reply somberly. "She's heartbroken. I can feel it." I rap at my chest, lips thinning as I stalk away from the liquor. "But she doesn't want me near her."

Xander takes a step towards me, the lines of concern on his face deepening. "That's not true, Ryatt. The soulmark—"

"It's not about the soulmark," I reprimand him sharply, "it's about *her*. What she wants and what she needs right now. Not what the bond wants. Or the wolf. Quinn wants space, needs it, so that's what she'll get until she tells me otherwise."

"You're going to leave her to deal with her grief alone?" he asks a bit apprehensively.

"Everyone is entitled to grieve in whichever way they choose, so yes," I growl, "If that's what she wants to do, so be it. It's the least I can do." *Even if it kills me to do so.* I clear my throat. "The witches are manning the borders to keep up the wards. They'll join the two crystals when the full moon makes its mark in the sky."

"I'll have wolves sent to join them. I suppose they're expecting trouble since the Wselfwulfs are involved." He frowns at my nod. "Very well. I shouldn't be too surprised. Carrie and her mother are almost as power hungry as Rollins."

"Yes," I murmur thoughtfully, "especially considering they're searching out the Amethyst of the Aztecs for a certain vampire. Or so the witches think."

Xander remains stoically silent for a moment. A tremor runs over his body before he delivers his terse reply. "Explain." I relay the meeting's happenings succinctly, watching impassively as Xander paces the length of the study.

"We'll deal with the ring after the crystal is settled," he tells me resolutely. "You'll stay with Quinn," he continues. I glare at the order. "You won't be needed out there. You're needed here. *With Quinn.*"

"I'm the Third. I should be out there. Besides, it's a full moon. If anyone needs to shift, it's me." I tap at my skull petulantly. "I can't afford to keep myself chained up for another month."

Xander crosses his arms over his chest and shakes

his head. "The witches' wards haven't been broken yet, and you'll manage," he tells me pointedly. "Focus on completing the soulmark with Quinn; that should keep your wolf busy." I bristle at the comment but hold back my retort. At least his last remark wasn't a full command.

"Are we through?" I ask tightly.

"I just want you to be happy, Ryatt," he tells me with a sigh, but nods and allows me to stalk away.

Quinn's just putting herself under the covers when I enter. She stills like a deer caught in headlights before reluctantly continuing, though her eyes remain on me as I step inside the room.

"Were you planning on sleeping in here?" she asks as I close the door behind me.

"If you'd allow it," I tell her, shuffling forward tentatively. She fidgets in the dark, which she may not be aware that I can see. Both blinds and curtains have been drawn on all the windows, leaving the room shrouded in mostly darkness. Yet I can see clear as day.

"After everything this week, I still found myself thinking at times that none of this was real. Vampires, witches, lycans; they don't exist. Soul mates and soulmarks don't exist. That it wasn't possible. It didn't matter that you had me and Zoelle take the truth serum, or that I've seen your eyes change from blue to gold at least a dozen times. Even after Zoelle's family's magic act I still caught myself doubting. There's always this little voice in the back of my head telling me it can't be real. But then I get that picture,"

Quinn sniffs, her voice beginning to shake, "and her throat was ripped apart. Literally torn open, and did you see her face? She looked so scared. So *horrified*. She had no idea about any of this supernatural bullshit, but I did. I could have warned her. I could have done something."

I ache to hold her in my arms, my feet bringing me to the edge of the bed before I can slam on the brakes. "It wasn't your fault, Quinn."

She shakes her head resolutely, somehow finding my eyes in the dark. "It is. I didn't have to involve her, but I did. I did because I was going to leave with her."

My heart halts and a pulse of pain radiates from my body. Quinn whines in response. "Why?" I croak, leaning a shaky hand on the bedpost.

"Because I don't want to be a prisoner here anymore," she whispers mournfully, "and I knew if I came back you would find some way to bind the soulmark." I shudder a sigh.

"I would never make you submit to the binding without your consent."

She lets out a wet bark of laughter. "That's not saying a lot considering how I was sealed and marked."

"I regret my actions, Quinn, more than you can know," I tell her earnestly. "I wouldn't force the binding on you. I swear it." She stills at my sincerity, her sniffling subsiding as she hastily wipes away the remnants of tears on her face.

"But would you let me go?" she asks. Another ripple of pain travels the length of my body. I gulp

185

down my nausea and nod.

"Yes," I respond hoarsely. "I would let you go." Even if it meant stalking her from the shadows for the rest of our days, just so that she wouldn't have to feel the pain of our separation.

"You would?"

Another nod she cannot see. "Yes, Quinn." Silence stretches between us, her face scrunching in contemplation.

"Then I'd like to leave. Today."

My grip tightens on the bedpost. "Not today." I continue before she can speak, her indignation spiking through the bond. "They're joining the crystal later today, and we expect the Wselfwulf Pack to cause trouble. It's not safe...but tomorrow, tomorrow you can leave if you wish."

Another silence. This one slowly tearing my heart apart as Quinn fidgets with the covers. "Alright," she finally whispers. I can tell she expected more of a fight, but I cannot bear to argue with her. "Tomorrow then."

CHAPTER 13

- Quinn -

I wake up sometime in the evening, Ryatt resting peacefully at my side. How we both slept so long is beyond me. He had nearly retreated after the declaration of my intent, but I had stopped him. The word "wait" having bolted past my lips before I could think to stop them. He had turned around with such hope written across his face I couldn't stand to devastate him once again like I knew my earlier words had. The soulmark was softening my resolve to him, which made the need to leave all the more urgent.

I was tucked into his body. Our legs loosely entangled. Hands resting gently upon one another. As if sensing I've awakened, Ryatt slowly begins to come to. His fingers flex against my hip before pulling away to properly stretch. I hesitate, then carefully detach myself from the comfort of his warmth. Enough of my wall had been torn down in the past couple of days; I didn't need Ryatt slipping past my weak defenses.

"Why don't you stay in bed a little while longer," he asks, sleep still staining his voice. "I'm sure we can find a way to entertain ourselves."

There is a teasing lilt to his words, though they still carry a familiar dark promise to them. The soulmark pulses with awareness, but I find myself shaking my head and shifting away from the warmth of his body. He clears his throat and the bed dips on the other side.

"I doubt Zoelle is around to make us any treats, but the kitchen staff will no doubt be around. How about I grab us something to eat and bring it back up here?" he suggests, discreetly adjusting his waistband as he walks towards the bedroom door. My eyes track his movements.

"I'll come with," I tell him just as his hand turns the doorknob. "We can eat downstairs." He gives a nod and a small smile, opening the door with his usual flair.

"After you," he murmurs.

I scoff as I pass, though it is halfhearted as his gaze follows me. "Don't think I don't know you just want to check out my ass." He grins rakishly in response.

"Me? Never." My returning grin halts halfway as the previous night comes into focus. "Hey," his hand reaches out to grab hold of my chin, "it wasn't your fault, Quinn. You could never have known that Vrana would have gone after your friend. In fact, it's quite odd that he was able to figure out her role in our plot so quickly."

I shake my head dully, escaping his gentle hold easily enough. "She's done jobs for him before. He's familiar with her work."

"I see."

We walk silently to the dining room, my stomach grumbling as I wait for him to return with our food. It gives me ample time to dissect the mess of thoughts colliding together in my head. Why had I agreed to wait? The longer I was around him the more I...*felt*. And feeling was something I desperately didn't want to do right now. I could learn to live with the guilt of M's death, but I wasn't sure if I could do it with Ryatt's constant empathy or that of the pack, which I could feel sifting its way through the bond. I wasn't sure how to handle it, and that's what I disliked most of all.

"I hope you like ice cream," Ryatt announces, coming in with two bowls of iced dairy goodness. The vanilla is barely seen under the obscene amount of chocolate that has been poured over both. I desperately want to put on some character to hide behind, but his rather ridiculous choice in food keeps plain old Quinn in place.

"Ice cream for dinner?" I ask, amused. He sits down next to me with a happy sigh.

"I like to live dangerously," he says, scooting his chair closer to mine. I can barely fend off the blush that douses my cheek and take a spoonful of the treat in minor defense.

"Where is everyone?" I ask once I've swallowed and Ryatt is busy with a mouthful of chocolate and ice cream.

"Out at the borders, no doubt," he informs me, words cutting a bit too sharply. "They're piecing the crystal back together, which will take a lot of magic and leave the witches vulnerable. If the crystal isn't put together, or the wards fall along the border, then the wolves are needed there to protect them."

"But not you?"

His smile turns slightly bitter. "Not I. I've been ordered to stay behind...with you." I catch his sidelong glance and find my breath caught in my throat.

"Why?"

"My brother hopes I'll be able to convince you to stay," he admits slowly. Though his tone is light, and his expression mirrors it, something behind his eyes is daringly hopeful. "But I certainly don't harbor any illusions that you will. Tomorrow we'll see you off, with an escort, mind you. I won't be deterred from that," he tells me sharply. "They know your face. Until you can slip away unnoticed someone will follow you at a distance. Probably Keenan." I let my spoon fall with a clatter.

"Not Keenan," I say seriously.

He eyes me surreptitiously. "Definitely Keenan."

"Why him? Why not some other wolf lackey? Keenan is pretty hard to miss."

Ryatt sends me a quick wink, "He's quite sneaky actually. One of our sneakiest wolves, I dare say."

"You're not actually going to have someone tail me, are you?"

His face turns serious. "I am. Keenan will know

190

who to look out for to make sure you aren't being tailed by someone from the Wselfwulf Pack, or to protect you from a vampire."

"I thought you were going to let me go?" I ask, heart strung tightly as I say the words.

He nearly growls back, strikes of lightning flashing in his eyes. "I am." A look of frustration passes across his face. His cheeks grow hollow as he takes in a steadying breath. "Despite how desperately I might want you or how painful it will be for both of us for you to leave, I won't make you stay. But you're still my soulmark. I won't let you go unprotected when the supernatural world is holding its breath waiting on the outcome of this day."

"What do you mean?"

"The Adolphus Pack and the Trinity Coven have been the talk of the town ever since we took on the Wselfwulf Pack together. Our alliance is unusual as the supernatural community prefers to stay close to their own. Vampires with vampires. Witches with witches. Lycans with lycans. We don't tend to mingle. Even the shape shifters and otherworldly creatures don't bother each other. If Zoelle wasn't Xander's soulmark, I doubt we'd still be here today."

A rather simple *"oh"* is all I can manage to muster. "Is there some kind of special Facebook group for supernaturals to use, where they can gossip about all the news and politics?"

"It happens easily enough through word of mouth. We tend not to lend our secrets to the vulnerability of the Internet." I hum accordingly and turn my

191

attention back to the ice cream. Ryatt's mouth opens as if to say more, but his phone lets out a series of chirps. He frowns and reaches for it.

"What is it?" I ask, going for nonchalant since Ryatt holds his phone just out of view.

"They're preparing the union of the crystal, and the Wselfwulfs have been spotted in the distance."

My eyes widen and search for a clock. "But the moon shouldn't be out for hours still."

Ryatt lets a rueful smile spear across his face. "You're right; it won't. There's no point in them arriving early, like they did last time. We'll be safe unless the ward falls, and if it doesn't, they'll scurry back home with their tails between their legs."

"What happens if the ward falls?"

"A bloodbath," he tells me darkly, "one I'll be missing." He scoffs and takes a spoonful of ice cream spitefully. I raise an incredulous brow.

"You want to be out there fighting?"

He mirrors my incredulous look. "Of course I want to be out there fighting! This is the one night of the month I can shift and it just so happens to coincide with a potential battle." He bops me on the nose with his spoon, startling me back at his juvenile action. "Of course I want to be there. Think of the glory of it all." His hand reaches out next and presses firmly beneath my chin, closing my mouth with a snap.

"Men," I mutter. "If you want to go, then go. I'm not stopping you."

"I can't," he repeats, ire clear. "I've been ordered to stay back with you."

I sigh and wipe the remnants of ice cream off my nose. "Did he say to stay back, or to stay with me?" Ryatt takes a moment to consider my words, then promptly grabs my face and kisses it.

"You're a genius," he whispers against my lips happily. Taken aback once more, my eyelashes flutter open a second later, my breath catching just so on a shaky exhalation. His eyes alight with mirth and the telltale anticipation that comes with finding the perfect loophole. It's a look I know well. One I have worn often. I swallow and push away the emotion, but give him a shy smile in return. Then he takes my hand, and we go.

+++

"I'm glad we changed before we left, but I wish we would have put on bug spray before leaving. I'm getting eaten alive out here," I complain. I've only one pair of shoes suitable for a trek in the forest: my pink Nike runners.

"You're about to witness something quite spectacular; you do realize that, yes?" He continues to lead me into the thick of the forest, every so often sniffing the air. His brother would be furious, he claimed, if he got wind that Ryatt had come out. Let alone with me tagging along behind him.

"You're really going to change in front of me?" I ask dubiously.

"*Shift*," he stresses.

"Whatever." He gives my hand a squeeze and

193

continues on silently, but I catch the amused smirk that finds his lips. It makes my heart skip a beat, and I wonder faintly for the millionth time how I'm going to leave when I keep letting myself be pulled in by his smiles and eyes. By his candor and wild side. *Ugh.* I shouldn't have come out here with him. Shouldn't have even hinted at it in the first place. But I couldn't deny that there was a part of me wanting to see him transform.

"Here," he says, coming to a standstill and inhaling the air deeply. "Any further and someone is bound to catch my scent or yours downwind."

I roll my eyes. "Well, obviously," I joke, but then he is stripping off his shirt and handing it to me. I take a startled step backward. "What the hell are you doing?" I ask, watching in shock as he starts on his belt and toes off his shoes.

"I'm not going to ruin a perfectly good pair of clothes by shifting in them. They'll get shredded," he tells me as if *I'm* the crazy one. When his pants drop my eyes close, though why I cater to his modesty when he has none is beyond me. "It's nothing you haven't seen before, sweetheart," he whispers close to my ear. I give a yelp and turn around wide-eyed, but he is no longer where I would have guessed him to be beside me.

A sudden cracking sounds from behind. Like the breaking of bones —an unforgiving and constant snapping and cracking and crunching.

I forget to breathe as my mind skids to a halt. Do I dare turn around? Fear grapples with my curiosity until a vicious snarl leaves me no choice but to spin round on my heel.

I fall to my knees, watching in a mixture of astonishment and horror as Ryatt's body lengthens and realigns. Another choked snarl and a crescendo of bones splintering into place, Ryatt falls to all fours. For a brief moment I see vestiges of the man he was, and in the next, his skin is pulling taunt over bone to become something else. His body vibrates with unrestrained energy before fur erupts from his stretched flesh. It sheaths his body in a sandy coat.

The shaking continues. The wolf's head twisting erratically from side to side as its snout finishes forming. Its lips pulling back to reveal pointed canines. An unsteady breath passes by my lips as I watch the transformation come to its end. Where once was a man, now stands a wolf.

"Holy shit," I whimper, squeezing my eyes tightly shut. Everything was true. *Everything.* My hands move to cover my face. Hiding me from the truth I had been so desperately running from. Something cold and wet presses against the back of my hands and slowly I let them fall. I lock gazes with the familiar golden eyes of Ryatt's wolf.

My hand ghosts upwards across the rough muzzle, aware that my every movement is being watched carefully. Up close I see how his fur coat is underlined with streaks of brown and tan. My fingers tangle in the coarse hairs about his neck and chest.

"You're..." Ryatt lets out a whine and lies down, placing his large head in my lap. My hands continue to

stroke the fur, marveling at the sheer size of him. The
wolf snuffs against my stomach. The heat of his breath
almost burning me clean. "...Beautiful." His tail gives
a lazy wag, tongue lolling out to give my leg a lick. We
stay like this for some time. Me, marveling at what
can no longer be denied. Ryatt the wolf peacefully
resting upon me.

A faint buzzing sounds in the air, but it takes some
time before either of us acknowledges the noise as
something electronic and not of nature. My hands
grope for his pants that lie nearby and track down his
phone.

"I don't know your passcode," I tell him, and wave
the phone in front of his face. The wolf huffs and
begins to stand, another whine treading on its vocal
cords. "I have an idea of what it could be though," I
inform him with a coy smile. "I've watched you type it
in enough times over the past week to get an idea. You
focus here, in the bottom left, then end right. Most
people choose a birthday or an arbitrary four number
combo, but you always punch in five." The wolf sits up,
staring at me very intently as I continue to ramble.
"I'm going to take a guess and say your code is 7-8-4-6-
6." The key lock screen vanishes after the final
number and I stand triumphantly. "Ha! I knew it!
Quinn: 7-8-4-6-6. You idiot. You hack all my files and
then put my name as your passcode. *Amateur.*"

The wolf takes a few steps away from me,
shuddering like he's undergone some violent seizure,
and then the snapping sounds again. The fur recedes.
The bones contract and snap back into their proper

place. Yet this time, no noise escapes him. No growls. No snarls. Not even a whine. All the sound that carries is his deft transformation back to his human form. He pulls to a grotesque height for one startling moment—his limbs too long, his spine unsure as it twists about—and then he is a man once more. Yet his golden eyes remain steadily upon me.

"Give me that," he heaves, hand outstretched, the serious look he wore as a wolf still somehow translating onto his face. But all I can stare at is his...

"Your pants?" I ask breathlessly. He snatches the phone from my hands and turns his back to me to read it, pacing forward. The muscles of his leg and derrière flex deliciously with each movement. I feel the air around us seize for the briefest of moments and unconsciously I find myself biting my bottom lip. The sensation is a tantalizing reminder of our steamier moments together: Mexico, the hallway, his bedroom, and the most lucid wet dream I had ever experienced. The air grows electric, and I can feel a heat spread through me as the memory lights my skin on fire. When had it become so easy to become lost in the mere sight of him?

"We need to go," he snaps, turning around towards me. Ryatt's face is torn in an angry scowl. It deepens upon further inspection of my current state. Eyes dilated. Face flushed. Heartbeat racing faster and faster by the minute. "What's wro—" he inhales deeply, eyes widening then narrowing in on me. *Lord have mercy.*

"If there were time," he tells me slowly, stalking

197

towards me with sordid intent. "I'd have you up against one of these trees moaning my name 'til your legs gave out."

He stands inches away from me, staring down at me with those golden eyes full of desire. A hand trails from my neck carefully along my collarbone, and he leans in infinitesimally closer. "And then I'd take you on the forest floor until you begged me for more," his tongue darts out to wet his bottom lip. The feel of his calloused fingers winds an unforgivable tension inside of me. One that begs to be snapped. "But I won't," he tells me without a hint of malice or bitterness, "because even though your body and the soulmark are screaming at you that you want to, I know that here," his fingers reach out to graze my heart, then up to brush along my temple, "and here, you're not ready." My breath leaves me in a whoosh as he takes a step back. He dresses in record speed, leaving me little time to compose myself.

"Where are we going?" I ask numbly, swallowing down the hurt of rejection I have no right to feel. My stomach clenches uncomfortably with guilt. My friend was dead because of me, and here I was lusting after some man. *Except he wasn't just some man, was he?* The traitorous thought does nothing to ease my shame. Ryatt's eyes narrow.

"The Baudelaires' house."

+++

The sun is sinking gradually in the west, the night

air turning cool as we race in Ryatt's BMW something-
series towards the Baudelaires'. I keep my eyes
trained out the front window for the entirety of the
ride, keeping count of how many glances Ryatt steals.
He had just reached 17 when we pull along a
somewhat familiar tree-lined street. Each house
boasts neatly trimmed yards and shiny new paint jobs.

"Are you going to tell me why they wanted us to
come over?"

Ryatt's grip tightens on the wheel. "The moon has
risen, you can see it—just over there." He points out
my window, and sure enough, there it is. Its' pale glow
trickling past the treetops. "They've joined the crystals
and the border is secure."

"That was fast," I say, a semblance of disbelief
clouding my voice.

"It was either going to work, or it wasn't," he tells
me, pulling to a stop in front of the familiar
craftsman-style two story.

"And it worked?" He nods, though I can sense his
hesitation, both through the bond and his body
language. "What aren't you telling me?" I ask quietly,
hand stilling on the seatbelt release.

"Something rather unexpected happened," he tells
me, undoing his seatbelt.

"What?"

He gives a short sigh of frustration, his brow
pinching together in thought. "A girl appeared after
the crystal was joined."

"A girl appeared?"

"Yes."

199

I pause, then ask tentatively, "From where?"

"That would be the question," Ryatt says on a sigh, exiting the car. I scramble after him.

"Are you seriously trying to tell me that some chick just '*poofed* into existence?'" Ryatt gives me a tight smile and places a hand on my lower back.

"I don't know the full details, but I've been told not to be, and I quote, 'A creep.' Something about not wanting to frighten the girl." Ryatt opens the door with an eye roll, steering me inside before him and towards the kitchen.

"Holy fuck," I breathe, eyes widening at the sight that greets me. I receive several pointed glares. "Sorry," I mutter, shifting back slightly as I take in the mysterious woman. She has a blanket wrapped loosely around her naked figure, though it does little to hide the more fascinating aspects of her features. My eyes are torn between tracing the iridescent wings materializing from her back and the vines and flowers gently winding beneath the surface of her skin. Her hair is a startling white, cut bluntly to hang just above her shoulders. She turns to look at us, purple eyes wide with a mixture of fright and curiosity.

"Hello," she says tentatively. I give her a small smile, nudging Ryatt to do the same with an elbow to the ribs. She smiles brilliantly back and thrusts a hand out towards us. "Would you like to shake hands?" she asks excitedly, the blanket dropping from her loosened hold. "Or would you prefer to kiss on the cheeks?"

My hand slaps over Ryatt's eyes and the woman

looks mildly offended at my reaction. She turns back to the witches "Did I do it wrong?" Zoelle is there in the next instant, wrapping the blanket back around her, face aflame.

"Just, don't forget to keep the blanket up, okay?" she says rather breathlessly.

"But it itches," she complains, a cross look covering her petite features. "I never have to wear anything in the Hollow Woods."

"You aren't in the Hollow Woods anymore, sweetheart," Maureen coos from nearby. "But don't you worry, we'll get you back there." The woman's lip trembles, eyes welling with tears before she throws herself at Ryatt. He stumbles back, eyes opening comically wide as her arms wrap around him and the blanket falls again.

I gasp, but soon find myself having to hold back a laugh at the alarm on his face. The woman sobs into Ryatt's chest, foot stomping every once in a while to demonstrate her displeasure.

"There, there," he mutters uncertainly, gently patting her atop her head. She turns her face upwards, eyeing Ryatt hopefully. "If Maureen says she'll get you back, she will." She nods her head, sniffling lightly before stunning the room with another of her smiles.

"You're so kind," she breathes, reaching up a hand to stroke his face. Ryatt looks at me in a panic, and I too find myself stilled with sudden...jealousy?

"Why...thank you," he replies, gently taking both of her wrists and stepping out of her hold. I pick up the blanket and thrust it into the woman's chest. She looks at me in alarm, but I have my most saccharine smile on. Her eyes flicker with uncertain confusion, then she pulls her lips into a disgruntled pout, adjusting the blanket reluctantly.

"I don't like it here. Everyone acts so confusingly. Saying one thing but their bodies saying another. All of my friends in the Hollow would never dream of treating each other this way. I just want to go home. Can't you send me now?" she pleads, sadness sinking back into her voice. "I don't belong here. I belong in the Hollow."

I insert myself into Ryatt's side and soften my posturing. The room stays oddly silent at her words, mournful expressions passing between the older women.

"What happened?" Ryatt asks, his eyes turning Xander's way. The Alpha stands at the kitchen window silently; eyes turned out towards the forest.

"Ask the witches," he quips. Diana sighs, rolls her shoulders back, and begins.

+++

The Earth was displeased. The air nearest the Elder Triad sizzled with magic and barely restrained energy as the remainder of the Trinity Coven—spread throughout the forest—implored the Earth to settle. It was the joining of such an unnatural item that brought about its displeasure. The Crystal of Dan Furth was not meant for the likes of this world, yet

*somehow, centuries ago, the object had been smuggled
across the planes of one world to the next. Witches
around the world coveted the crystal for its powerful
properties, but seldom few could be trusted with its
care. Indeed, the splitting of the crystal was in part
due to a band of unfit witches. With the crystal
halved, the Earth new no worry of what unnatural
acts could prosper from its magical powers. Until now.*

*"The crystal," Diana Baudelaire bids her
granddaughter and another witch forward. The two
approach the small circle the coven elders create, yet
their carefully measured steps are laborsome. Each
witch holds her hands outstretched, palms flat and
facing forward, steering the crystal into the circle.
Their struggle is clear. The very presence of the Earth
urging them back even as they trudge forward. The
crystal halves quiver in either excitement or detest.
No one is certain, yet the witches continue. The
crystals pass by the interlinked arms of the elders.*

*Maureen Clybourn lets her head tip back, her long
white hair stirring in the growing wind that encircles
the trio. Her skin carries the weight of the last
encounter involving the crystal. Devilish red patches
scarring her alabaster flesh. She takes the lead, her
voice a whisper as the two crystals hover uneasily
within the band of their circle.*

*Diana and Lydia's heads follow suit, their necks
bent at an almost unusual angle as Maureen's words
grow louder.*

"Ad lucem. Ad mortem. Qui semper."

The spell is taken up on the wind and soon the

*invocation begins to tumble from the mouth of each
witch present. One by one the words grow into a litany
of hoarse cries that build and fall with the growing
wind.*

*Howls echo from afar; the Wselfwulf Pack
responding. Wolves dot the tree line, a smattering of
golden eyes piercing the darkening forest. The
Wselfwulf Pack was ready and waiting with barely
restrained contempt for the Trinity Coven to fail and
fall to ruin. Along with their sworn enemies, the
Adolphus Pack, that dare side with them.*

*The air splinters. Visible fissures of light sparking
in a shockwave along the poorly held magical border
protecting the Adolphus Pack's claimed territory. The
wolves stiffen. Each side standing with hackles raised,
and horrible gnashing teeth bared. The Wselfwulf
Pack prowls forward. There is a palpable electricity to
the air, riding high on a fine tension that is on the
cusp of breaking. The witches slowly rise from the
ground. One perilous inch at a time as their words are
lost to the swell of wind sweeping them upwards. The
crystal halves shine brighter and brighter as they near
each other, until with a sharp and distinctive* **crack,**
they collide.

*The border shatters; the wolves advance, and a
new light appears. The witches of the Trinity Coven
fall to the ground, spent of their magic and
defenseless. Yet the body of light that remains shines
brighter. Grows larger. The Wselfwulf Pack hesitates,
and in doing so, is spared their lives. The light takes a
corporeal form, and with it, a new barrier erects itself*

in a brief prism of colors.

The woman who remains standing is unearthly beautiful with snow-white hair and wings that gleam like opals. Beneath the surface of her skin roams a seemingly never-ending track of vines spouting leaves and pale flowers. The woman's wings fold themselves neatly against her bare back as she splays a hand tentatively against the wall she has created. Her violet eyes growing wide as she takes in the scene before her. Rokama surround her. Or something frighteningly similar for they lack the telltale markings of the rokama she knows. No obsidian eyes or red-stained muzzles. No leathery, wings jutting from the spine. The new creature squeezes her eyes closed. Rokama or not, these beasts would not bring her harm. Nor the innocents fallen too her left and right.

Taking a deep breath she opens her eyes and meets the golden gaze of some beast across the way. It sounds a savage bark, the pack around it echoing the reprimand. The woman's fists clench against her side, a blinding fury growing inside her chest. The flora dances beneath her skin, further winding her defenses.

A second later and the Adolphus Pack would have found themselves at the mercy of the strange creatures fur—if not for their Alpha. The largest of the wolves, he steps in front of the strange woman with a threatening snarl directed at the Wselfwulf Pack.

The winged-woman stares flabbergasted at the act. Mouth comically held open, as the anger simmering inside her stalls at her throat. The act is not enough to earn her full trust, but it is enough—enough to spare those who stand with her on the east side of the barrier. She walks to the wolf's side. Anger flooding her once more like some wild rapid. She has never been very good at controlling the swing of her emotions.

Too bad for the Wselfwulf Pack.

The Alpha lets out a whine and takes a tentative step back as the earth starts to shake. The Wselfwulf Pack scatters. Startled yelps and barks sounding as vines jut from the forest floor and begin to impale those not fast enough to escape. It is a bloodbath. A frenzied chaos that ends only when the woman lets out a piercing scream. The Earth shivers at the abrupt silence that follows, calming the forest floor with an eerie groan. The woman steps back and retrieves the Crystal of Dan Furth from the ground. She holds it to her breast as she sends a tentative, but warm smile to those who remain around her.

"Hello," she murmurs. Though she remains unsure as to where she is or how she came to be in this peculiar forest, she no longer feels afraid. Her smile turns brighter as she gazes down at the bewildered Elder Triad. "You may call me Luna."

+++

"The spell to rejoin the pieces worked just as planned," Diana finishes, her voice hard as if in reprimand to Xander's earlier tone.

206

"Did your plan involve her?" he asks briskly.

Diana visibly bristles. "No. We're looking into the matter as we speak." Xander says nothing, holding himself still at the window. "We aren't sure as to why joining the crystal would bring Luna to us."

"He's mad at me, isn't he?" the woman, Luna, asks. She fiddles with the blanket, her face scrunching up as it slides against her skin. Zoelle comes forward once more to help her adjust it.

"He's not mad at you," Zoelle tells her softly, "he's just confused."

"About what?"

"About you."

"Why?" Luna tilts her head to the side, fussing once more with the blanket as impatience darkens her tone. For one who is clearly a grown woman, she acts most decidedly like a child.

"Because he didn't realize you would be here," she explains carefully. "If he would have, we would have prepared."

"Oh."

Silence once more. No one seems to know what to say next, but I can feel my curiosity rising. As if sensing my shift in mood, Ryatt's grip tightens on my waist in warning. Like that was going to stop me.

"What are you?" I ask. Luna blinks.

"I'm a fairy," she says somewhat matter-of-factly. "What are you?" *Well, shit.*

"I'm a human." Luna looks at Ryatt, the flowers and vines beneath her skin slowing their winding path to a halt.

207

"He's not." I give a short laugh at her blunt words.

"He's a lycan, just like his brother." Luna stiffens and shuffles back towards Maureen.

"*Rokama*," she hisses, eyes darting nervously between the two men. "They cannot be trusted with the innocent. Come," she holds out a hand to me, "you should not be so close to danger."

Ryatt stiffens and his hold tightens. "He's not going to hurt me. Neither of them will, Luna."

"They're rokama," she tells me stubbornly, "like the others. They cannot be trusted."

"They're lycans, not rokama, and they are our *allies*, Lunaria," Diana tells her. "No harm will come to you while you are under our care. Nor theirs." The words do little to placate Luna, but she does cease her glaring and drop her hand.

"He doesn't hurt you?"

"No, Luna. Sometimes he can be a bit of a prick, but he's never deliberately hurt me. Except for a few incidents, that is..."

Ryatt flushes under my regard. "I apologized for that," he mutters.

"And you...forgave him?" My heart skips a beat under her scrutiny.

"I did," I reply slowly, almost unsure of the answer myself. Ryatt straightens. A sudden surge of happiness pulsates through the bond, leaving me glowing with strange satisfaction. "He's not so bad," I finish lamely.

"...You are in love?" she asks, equal parts curious and serious. I guffaw.

"She can barely keep her hands off me," Ryatt replies smoothly, squishing me into his side.

"Get over yourself," I grumble, struggling to push away from him, the smile I tried so hard to beat winning out.

"It's definitely love," he continues, keeping me within the circle of his arm. "I'm preparing a winter proposal and a June wedding. Expect an invitation in the mail."

"A union!" she squeals excitedly, clapping her hands together and bouncing about. "How joyous! Who would have thought a beast such as yourself could ever love, or be loved in return!"

The blanket falls to the floor in her glee, giving the entire room a show not easily forgotten.

CHAPTER 14
- Quinn -

"I can't believe fairies exist," I exclaim, climbing the stairs to Ryatt's bedroom. "I mean, I shouldn't be surprised because, hello, witches, lycans, and vampires are real, but *wow*. A fairy. Did you see her wings and her skin? Disney did *not* prepare me for this moment. Also, did you notice she has zero filter? Or how her mood jumps from one to another in about two seconds flat?"

Ryatt chuckles at my side, scratching the back of his neck. "I certainly wasn't expecting to see a fairy when we arrived. I'm just glad that the witches will be seeing to her care and not us. You're already quite the handful." He bumps me with his shoulder good-naturedly, opening the door to the bedroom and allowing me through first. I immediately kick off my sneakers and sit on the large chest at the end of the bed.

"I don't think she would have liked to have been

under the pack's care. What did she call you again?"

"A rokama," he says, slipping off his shoes as well and stretching out on the bed. "Whatever that is."

"She understood the word lycan enough to associate it with a rokama, so I'd assume something similar." Ryatt looks pensive for a fleeting second before it vanishes from his face and he sits up.

"I suppose you're right," he tells me somewhat cordially. "Well, I'm off for a bit. I'll just grab some of my things and leave you to the rest of your night."

"What?" My eyes follow Ryatt's stiff movements with astonishment. "Where are you going?"

"Out for a run."

"A run?" My insides twist at his flippant tone. A surge of indignation runs through me for no good reason at all. "Seriously?"

He stills, but it's momentary. "I'm not a masochist," comes his cold response. "You're leaving tomorrow. That's still your plan, correct?"

I nod my head numbly, swallowing the sudden lump in my throat. "Yes," I say meekly.

"You said you had forgiven me—earlier—was that true?" His back is still turned to me, hands stalled on his dresser drawer. I do not dare give my reply because it was true. Yet saying the words aloud once more would crumble the last of my resolve. Tomorrow I will leave and—I squeeze my eyes tightly shut—and do what? Go where? I didn't know, but it would at least be my choice. My decision.

My mistake, a voice whispers darkly in my mind.

It will all be mine. Ryatt slams the dresser drawer

211

shut, tossing his things in a duffle bag he's taken from the closet.

"I don't get you," he tells me quietly. "This evening in the forest. It was just you and I out there. You didn't wear any of your masks, and it was *good*, Quinn. You know I can feel it through the bond? Your true feelings towards me? But you'll happily go on denying them so that you can what, have the last word? Save your pride?"

"That's not it, Ryatt. You don't—"

"—I don't what?" He stares me down, swinging the bag over his shoulder as he pins me with a searing glare. "*Understand?* You're right. I don't. I know this whole scenario is one big cluster-fuck and that I went about it all wrong, but there are times when it seems like none of it even matters to you. Like you don't seem to care about it as much as you let on. Quinn, I know I can make you happy. I've never been so in sync with someone, and I know the same is true for you. But you'll forsake it all just to save face."

"That's not true," I tell him painfully, itching to stand and declare my growing feelings for him. Yet I stay firmly planted in my seat, not daring to lose myself to these strange feelings.

He growls, "Then why?"

"Because," I choke, "this is all too much, alright? This whole supernatural, paranormal world. I don't belong here."

"And yet, somehow, you manage to get along famously with my sister, a she-wolf, and Zoelle and her merry band of witches. You do fit in here. You're just making excuses. You belong with me. Here." My heartbeat thunders in my ears as I watch him stalk towards the door. "The fact of the matter is, for all your bravado and games, you're scared. You're scared of love, Quinn. The love that could be between us, and the love the people in this town could give to you if you'd just let them try." I watch wordlessly as he leaves, heart shattering into a million pieces.

Game and match: Ryatt.

+++

"You're an idiot," Irina remarks coldly as I toss my luggage in the trunk of my car. I send her a pageant queen smile and slam the trunk closed.

"I'm not."

"Whatever little argument you had last night doesn't matter, you fool. You have literally found your soul mate, and you're just going to walk away from that? That might as well be the very definition of idiocy."

"I'm not going to argue about this with you," I tell her frankly, stepping up to the driver side door and facing off against her chilling glare.

"Where are you going to go? The Wselfwulfs know who you are, and Vrana is most certainly out for your blood."

"Ryatt said someone would be watching out for me until I could make a clean getaway."

Irina scoffs, coming up and slamming my door shut as I begin to open it. "You're not just breaking his heart you know? You're turning your back on the Pack too, and they certainly haven't done anything to deserve this." I gently push her hand away and open the door again.

"I have your number. I'll keep in touch." She scoffs and turns heel, marching off back towards the house. Adjusting my sunglasses, I slip into the driver's seat, shutting the door with a sharp clip. Irina was the only one to see me off. If it could be even called that. No Ryatt, or other members of the Adolphus pack. Not even Zoelle. To say it didn't hurt a little would have just been one more lie to add to the pile I had accumulated. Before I can lose my nerve, I put the car in reverse and peel out of the driveway into the street, gunning my way out of the town.

It's not long into my drive before I feel my stomach twist itself into painful knots. My breath begins to come in panicked waves, the early vestiges of hyperventilation, as I reflect on the choice I've made. Before I can quite comprehend what I am doing, my car ends up in front of the Baudelaire home. Zoelle had mentioned something about a tea to keep her feelings under control. To numb the bond. I would just pick some up before I left. Smoothing back my hair and checking my face in the mirror, I exit the car and head to the front door.

"Oh!" My hand is poised to knock when the door is unceremoniously yanked open.

"Oh, indeed." Lydia Stein lets her eyes flick over me, a knowing gleam inside them as she breezes past. "You're not likely to find what you need in there, girl, but you can try." These witches were definitely mind readers. No matter what Zoelle said.

"Are they in the kitchen?" I ask. She directs a nod over her shoulder, leaving the door wide open for my entrance.

"Shut the door and come in, child." I do as I'm told, following Diana's voice and finding her, Maureen, and Luna in the kitchen. Luna wears a dark denim shift dress that does nothing to flatter her figure. It's at least two sizes too big, though; with her almost size zero frame I doubted anything Zoelle, or even I had, could fit her.

"Hi."

Diana raises a cordial brow. "There's no need for sunglasses in here. Go on and take those off and have a seat."

"I just came to grab some tea. I really need to get on the road."

"*Sit.*" I'm not quite as mentally prepared as I should be for this kind of standoff, but I couldn't walk away now. I take off my sunglasses reluctantly, taking a seat near Luna. She watches our exchange raptly, eyes glued to me as I sit.

"What?" I ask curtly, unable to knock the edge from my voice. I wasn't so sure I'd be able to keep my cool with the loose-lipped fairy.

"You've been crying," she tells me matter-of-factly. "Why?"

I grit my teeth. "I haven't been crying."

Luna's eyes widen in surprise and she looks to the two elder women for guidance. "She lied to me!"

215

"I did not," I say tactfully. "I—"

"Yes, you did. You said you hadn't been crying, but you have." Maureen sets a steaming cup of tea in front of me.

"It's best to be honest with Luna. She's like a supernatural bloodhound. She can sniff out a lie a mile away."

Just great. "How precious."

"It has its advantages," Diana counters. "What kind of tea are you looking for?"

I clear my throat. "Something to stem the bond. Zoelle said she used it when she was with Xander, and it helped."

"She's lying again," Luna says in confusion, scrunching her brow. "Why does she lie so much?"

I take a deep breath and count to five slowly. "Would you mind keeping the commentary to a minimum, Luna? The big girls need to have a chat." Luna looks put out but obliges. Sitting back in her seat, she crosses her arms over her chest.

"We have something, though I'm sure it won't do you any good. You're much too far gone for anything we have to help."

"Seriously?" I take the news like a punch to the stomach, breath hitching as sorrow stretches across my being.

"You've consummated your relationship before completing the soulmark. This act binds you in a different way to Ryatt."

"Fuck me," I groan, pinching the bridge of my nose.

"You shouldn't curse," Luna says haughtily.

I turn a glare her way. "Well, you shouldn't talk. Ever." Luna's purple eyes shade darker, almost to black, as she glares back at me.

"You're very rude for a person in love." I gape at her in response, though I catch Maureen and Diana passing a sly smirk to each other.

"I'm not in love," I tell her sternly. She pouts some more.

"You might as well be," she snarks back, "He certainly loves you. Though it's a wonder why."

"Quinn here prefers a life of solitude," Diana tells Luna before I can make my retort. "That's why she's going away. Isn't it Quinn?" I nod my head reluctantly.

"But he loves her," Luna says uncertainly, losing her bite. "Is he going with you?"

I shake my head. "I don't think you understand what the word solitude means."

"Why would you leave him if he loves you and if you're falling in love with him? That doesn't make sense."

"What can I say," my words brittle and tight, "I'm full of surprises."

She looks at me seriously. "Why?"

"Why what?" I ask back, frustration blooming inside my chest. I turn my gaze back to the older women. "Can I have the tea still? Anything is better than nothing."

"I'll mix some up for you," Maureen tells me, moving slowly to one of the kitchen cabinets. Her movements are slightly shaky, and a grimace flickers over her face at the simple action. "I can feel your pity from here. I don't need it. I'll be fine in no time. The spell just took a lot out of me."

Luna's lips thin and I catch her eye. "Lie," she mouths. My lips quirk upwards, but only slightly.

"We have something akin to soulmarks in the Hollow. You see, every fairy is created with their match in mind, and a sigil placed upon them to help find their match. Most fairies find their match shortly after their conception, as they're typically wrought from the same field."

"How exactly are fairies...conceived?" I ask, mind stunned to a standstill for a brief moment.

Luna blinks owlishly back at me. "Why, we come from flowers of course." She gives a short burst of laughter, her mirth evident at my lack of knowledge. "How else would we be conceived?"

I let out an unladylike snigger. "Oh, *trust me*, there are more fun ways to *conceive*."

"Are you speaking of the pleasures of the flesh?" The sip of tea I take is spat out immediately, half ending up back in the cup while the other spills down my chin.

"Oh my God."

"Lunaria, we spoke about this earlier. Topics such as pleasures of the flesh are not to be had in polite company," Diana chides. Luna flushes apologetically.

"Your name is Lunaria? As in the plant that forces you to tell the truth?" Maureen sits down beside me and gives my knee a gentle pat.

"I was born of the Lunaria!" Luna tells me

218

brightly. "What flower did you come from?"

I grin. "The pink lotus."

"Do not encourage her, Quinn Montgomery," Diana reprimands sharply.

"That sounds like a very pretty flower," she says. "I'm sure I've seen it before in the Hollow." I hum my agreement.

"It most certainly is."

"That's enough, Quinn. Don't you have somewhere to go?" Diana sends me a pointed look that makes me cringe internally. *Time's up.* I stand up and give a weak smile to both Maureen and Luna. Maureen presses a soft silk pouch into my hand.

"Steep for two to three minutes. No more." I nod.

"You're really leaving?" Luna exclaims unhappily. Again I nod. "But—but doesn't he make you happy?"

"He does—

"And doesn't he complement you?" she continues earnestly.

"I wouldn't call them compliments so much as lecherous come-ons."

Luna frowns. "...I do not think you understand," she murmurs, "Does he *complement* you?" I give pause to the notion, thinking of his corny jokes and well-timed wit. The way we play together and play off each other.

"Sort of," I admit, finding my mouth a bit dry. "Maybe."

"And he loves you," she states. My gaze flicks uneasily from Luna's to the window behind her, my heart sounding out a rapid beat against my breast.

219

"He might."

"But you will leave him anyway?" A quizzical look falls upon her brow. I swallow.

"It's not safe for me here." Luna stares deeply into my eyes—as if she can see straight through me. See all my fears and past heartaches. And then she smiles gently, her wings briefly coming into focus behind her and catching in the sunlight. A kaleidoscope of colors spills onto the floor.

"You're never safe from the wants of your heart," she tells me kindly, "so what's the point in running?"

CHAPTER 15

"Where are you going?" Irina asks, irritation coating her voice as she watches Ryatt pass in a fluster.

"Out," Ryatt replies briskly, barreling past her towards the back of the house. Irina sighs, sipping on her iced coffee absentmindedly as she makes her way to the front door, eyes glued to the screen of her phone. The sharp rap of a car door closing sounds, followed closely by heels approaching on the driveway. It's all the warning Irina needs to step to the side. Eyes widened in interest, Irina watches as Quinn advances inside with a very determined swish of her hips.

"Where are you going?" Irina asks, hiding her delight at seeing the blonde again so soon. Quinn looks sharply to her left, eyes going large at the other woman's unexpected presence. "He's gone out," Irina tells her with a smug curl of her lips, "that way." Quinn's face colors lightly, even more so as Irina flounces off outside, shutting the door loudly behind her. Taking a steadying breath, she hardens her resolve once more and heads to the back of the house.

+++

Quinn

Where the fuck was he? I did not put on my Christian Louboutin booties to trudge through the dirty forest floor. These were strictly indoor shoes, which were meant to impress and entice illicit rendezvous. Not gather dirt and grime on the expensive leather.

"Ryatt!" I shout, stopping on more solid ground and scanning my surroundings. How had he not already heard me approaching? Or smelled my scent on the wind? He was supposed to possess supernatural abilities and be here already. I scan the forest expectantly, sucking in a deep breath to shout once more when—

"Quinn!" Ryatt exclaims, clearly out of breath. I turn around with a yelp and eye his disheveled appearance. Sans shirt and shoes, wearing a pair of basketball shorts. Skin glistening. He stares at me crossly. It is not the reaction I was hoping for.

"Out for a run?" I ask lightly, receiving no response but the tightening of his lips. "Without shoes, I see. Interesting choice." He doesn't answer right away, letting my anxiety grow unreasonably high.

"I wasn't expecting to see you back here," he finally responds, voice dipping into a low vibrato that raises the hair on my arms and neck. He steps cautiously forward, each step bringing him mindfully closer, yet staying just out of reach. I spot the look of heat that swirls behind his eyes and feel my heart skip a beat. "You must have known the implications of what that would mean." He stops inches from me, the weight of his regard drawing every inch of my skin to attention. My nipples tighten, and I find myself squeezing my thighs together.

Luna's parting words had struck a chord, and I had found myself unable to shake myself of them. For too long I had been frightened of relying upon another person. Of letting anyone in. In turn, I had closed myself off to the one thing my heart had wanted the most. Love.

I let out a shaky breath. I had stolen from witches and lycans, double-crossed a vampire, and somehow made it out alive. Maybe, just maybe, love wasn't the scariest monster out there. I feel my resolve firm. It was time to get my heart back in the game.

"I know what I'm doing," I whisper back.

"Do you?" he asks archly, but an undercurrent of lust seeps into his words. I shiver and force myself a meager step forward. Until there is only an inch between us. The old Quinn would have donned some new mask for this new adventure. She would have met Ryatt tit for tat and played as if it was a game. But the real Quinn, the one Ryatt seemed to bring out so effortlessly with his easy banter, was ready to relinquish control. *To live.*

A true smile graces my lips, though it is small in

stature. "I do," I tell him, feeling my heartbeat running through my veins. Something flashes behind his eyes: triumph, I realize. Gold slips through the haze of blue like flashes of lightning, his wolf pressing against the forefront of his mind, no doubt. Ryatt's hand slips to my waist, eyes half-lidded.

"I was going to follow you," he confesses, tugging me into his chest. He wears his own smile now. One that lightens the severe expression on his face. Finally. "I was never going to let Keenan watch over you."

"You love me," I tell him, smile brightening. "A fairy told me so." He hums his agreement, mirth sparkling in his eyes.

"Really? I suppose some might say...you've stolen my heart." I groan my displeasure while his laughter rings throughout the forest.

"That joke isn't funny, Ryatt. You are not funny."

He smiles down at me, his free hand coming up to caress the side of my face. "I am funny, and now you have the utmost pleasure of being able to enjoy it 24/7." I scrunch my nose in distaste, even as I laugh. As my mirth dies down his eyes flicker to my lips.

A beat goes by, then another. The air around us is charged with tension until I realize that I must make the first move for this to truly be my decision. I press my hands against his chest, feeling his heart racing nearly as fast as mine. It gives me the courage to reach up on my toes and place my lips decidedly across his. Instantly a flood of desire curls my toes. I moan into his mouth, enjoying far too much the way he kisses me back so ardently.

My hands lock around his neck to tug him closer, fingers grasping at the fine ends of his hair. There is a desperation between us. A hunger that strikes at my core—at my very being—that refuses to be denied any longer. His kiss consumes, and I succumb to the branding lash of his teeth and tongue. A moan breaks free from my lips. Calloused hands follow the curve of my hips upward until they reach their goal, lingering tantalizingly beneath my breast. They skirt the edges, denying me the pleasure of his touch until I feel them cupping my jaw, tilting my head back to kiss me deeper.

Ryatt pulls away with a strangled moan, his thumb reaching out to trace my swollen lips. "Do you like this dress?" he asks, leaning in and kissing each of my cheeks tenderly. I nod slowly, eyes fluttering open to read his expression. "My apologies then," he says, not sounding the least bit remorseful. His hands drop from my face to the collar of my dress and in the next instant, they have ripped it in two. Right down the middle. A $600 dress turned rag in under three seconds. I push away with a startled gasp.

"Ryatt!" He ignores my indignation, looking far too be pleased with his handiwork. "This is Michael Kors. You do not just rip a $600 Michael Kors dress in half."

He prowls forward, each step deliberately made to crowd me back. "I rather like the fashion statement it's making." My entire body feels flushed, and it only worsens at the dark intention of his voice. "If you don't wish the same fate for your undergarments, I suggest you take them off. Now."

I release a shaky breath as he circles me. Well aware that he is the predator, and I the prey. I shrug out of the ruined dress, letting it pool at my feet. Ryatt winds his way back to face me as I let my hands inch their way over my stomach and up to cup my breasts. His steps slow. Anticipation tingles at my fingertips as they edge the lining of my bra. Ryatt takes a step forward, eyes glued to my wandering hands until they stop at the silk bow placed front and center.

"This is what you wanted, right?" I ask breathlessly, pinching the fabric together and letting it fall open. The wolf snarls, the sound stemming from deep inside him as he stalks ever closer. The summer air slips over my newly released skin in a blanket of warmth. With a soft thud, my bra joins the ruined dress.

A fevered moan rides my next exhalation. My fingers reach to fondle my breasts. To twist and pinch the over sensitive peaks. Watching Ryatt on the cusp of losing control sends a dizzying thrill of power through me. To feel so wanted is a heady notion, but the look in his eyes is like no other, so full of violent desire. There would be no hiding anymore. No more running. I let a hand sink down past my navel to trace the lace of my panties. Another moan is ready at the edge of my tongue when he finally snaps.

I've barely time to blink before my back is against the rough bark of some tree, my thighs wrapped tightly around Ryatt's waist. Hands captured between his own.

"This," he breathes harshly against my ear, "is what I want." He bites at my earlobe and leaves a trail of marks down my neck. There is something primal in the way we move together. His absolute control and possession of my body nearly drive me over the edge. I bow my head back, enjoying the noise he releases at my surrender. We come together in unison, hips grinding against one another in search of release. The heat of my sex seeps through my panties as I rub myself against the hard bulge beneath his shorts.

Ryatt's name falls from my lips in a plaintive cry, back arching almost painfully as I thrust my breasts towards his attentive mouth. Blood pounds through my temples. It is the only other sound known to me outside our heady breaths. The feel of his lips, wet and hot, around my rosy peaks draws another cry. Ryatt is scorching to the touch. All parts of him. He burns a path from one peak to the next, lavishing it with unchained passion.

"Do you remember what I told you the other day?" he asks, the husky timbre of his voice sending shivers down my spine as he releases my hands. They fall to his shoulders, relishing in the way he caresses the length of my arm. The touch so soft it could be mistaken for a whisper. That is, until it buries itself in my hair and yanks my head to the side. I let out an angry hiss, hips jerking in shock, fingers locking down on their purchases. He bites and kisses at my jaw, thrusting back savagely with his hips and pressing me into the tree. "Do you?"

I let out a short whine at his rough attentions,

unable to deny the excitement it arouses within me.
"*Yes*," I hiss. The forest feels thick with silence as his
wicked smile grows against my skin. The moment
becomes almost unbearable the way it stretches on
into forever.

"Good."

He kisses me, lips claiming my own with renewed
fervor. I cannot seem to get enough of him. The way
his muscles twitch and contract under my frenzied
exploration. They grope the panels of his abdominals
and pectorals, relishing in the way in which they
contract so minutely. I am enraptured. Caught so
tightly within our passion, I feel as if it's choking me.
Ryatt's lips blaze a path down my neck once more,
lingering over the course of my collarbone. A whine
careens from my throat. I wanted more. I wanted this.
Ryatt, and everything that came with him.

My hands fall to the trim cut of his hips and push
at his shorts. A sudden desperateness to feel him
inside me replacing all other needs. Yet I have barely
accomplished my task when my hands are recaptured
and pinned above my head with but one of his.

"Say that you're mine," he pants into my ear, nails
scratching a dangerous path towards my hairline,
where the soulmark burns across my flesh.

"I'm yours," I whimper in reply, feeling the tip of
his hard shaft press against my panties. Lust holds
me in a chokehold; my entire body strung so tightly I
feel I might explode if he doesn't do something.
Anything. His hand falls to my shoulder. Down my
breast. Past my stomach to the last silk barrier

between us. It's gone with a flick of his wrist.

It happens quicker than I expect; his cock riding between my folds. The sensation draws a sharp stab of desire through us both. His head falls to my shoulder, hand trembling as it finds its way back to my throat. The fingers inch their way around to the nape. I suck in a startled breath as the broad head of his cock slips inside.

"Say that you'll bind yourself to me." His plea is a heated whisper running across my breastbone. Lips anchored to my clavicle. "*Please.*" A dart of fear spears my heart, stalling my immediate reply. *No more running*, I think. I push my hips down and let his thick member take another inch.

I tug my hands loose from his dominating grip, hands groping for his face to pull him towards my lips. With a shuddering breath I whisper my reply. "I bind myself to you."

Something inside me contracts, then expands like some kind of explosion. I cannot contain my gasp, for with it comes the sudden wide expanse of emotions between us crashing into me like a tidal wave. His hand cups the back of my neck and without further hesitation, he plunges himself deeply inside of me. My legs tighten, overcome with the reckoning of his need. For a moment, stars flash brilliantly before my eyes and I fall into a dark abyss where only he and I exist. My body moves along with his without a single thought, knowing one thing only: we are made to be one.

"Christ," he groans against my lips, kissing me

with such fervent ardor that I find myself on the verge of climax. There is no escaping this kiss. His tongue and lips possess me in nothing short of a primal claiming. Too soon my breath hitches, body tightening as his fingers dig almost painfully into my soulmark. My body shakes as it bucks back against every one of his thrusts. I release a sharp cry that echoes throughout the forest as my release crashes around me.

My legs begin to lose their grip about his waist, but Ryatt's hands are quick to catch me. "We're not finished," he purrs, roughly slamming into me. I suck in a hungry breath, dimly aware of the sharp presence of scratches along my naked back. The pain is minuscule in comparison to the pleasure still scoring my body.

"Please," I whimper, hardly knowing what I'm even asking for. He growls his acknowledgment, hands placed strategically underneath me as he keeps me pinned to the tree. His hips slow to a torturous pace so that he can rest his forehead against my own.

"It's alright," he pants, "I know what you want." *Thank God.* A look of determination flashes gold in his eyes, the pace of his hips increasing as well as my sounds of delight. The tightening comes again, raising the flesh across my skin as I hold on. Our moans chime together as our releases hit in harmony. My back scraping painfully against the tree as his hold slackens.

He pulls back, breathing harshly over me as my toes touch the ground unsteadily. The warmth of our union slides down my thighs, eliciting a shiver of delight.

"Ready?" he breathes after a long moment, tilting my head up and placing a soft kiss on my lips. I quirk a lazy smile.

"For what?" I breathe, unprepared for him to sweep me to the forest floor. "*Oomph!*" He looks entirely too pleased with himself above me, thigh nestled comfortably between my own.

"I do believe I mentioned something about this before," he teases, eyes twinkling merrily. His happiness soars through the bond, intertwining with my own. What remains of the wall around my heart shatter, a feeling I had once thought lost to me settling firmly into place. *So this was what it felt like to fall in love*, I think with a content smile. What adventures would it bring?

"You might just have to remind me," I reply coyly, a sudden shyness encapsulating me as my fingers fan themselves over his heart tenderly. The intimate act brings a soft smile to his face. Ryatt catches my hand and brings it to his lips.

"You won't regret this," he promises. I give him a brilliant smile. No. I most certainly wouldn't.

EPILOGUE

"I don't see what all the fuss is about," Ryatt mutters, watching us with a stormy frown in the doorway of our bedroom. Irina and I continue to hold up varying color palettes against the navy blue walls.

"You might have better style than Aleksander, dear brother, but that doesn't mean you have an eye for interior design," Irina states, eyes never leaving the color samples.

"That's because all that matters regarding the bedroom is the size of the bed," he sasses back, a sly grin curving upwards on his handsome face.

"Don't start," I warn, sending a scalding look over my shoulder. "If I'm going to live here I want it to feel like home, and I don't like dark color schemes like this. They're too moody."

"I rather think it sets the mood," he purrs, prowling into the room.

"For depression," Irina deadpans, delivering the same look to her brother. Ryatt halts, features ruffling back into the stormy frown.

"Isn't it time you moved out, little sister?"

She flutters her eyelashes at him, "Why I'd love to, brother dearest. Then I'll set about painting my room some dark and dreary blue to *set the mood* for all my *guests*." A thunderous expression flashes behind his eyes, lips thinning.

"You're not leaving this house until you're married," he promises darkly, sulking away.

"Such a drama queen," Irina murmurs, focus turned back onto an orangish-red color called Burnt Sienna. "How do you like this with the off-white trimming?"

"You're all drama queens," I'm quick to assure her, continuing before she can protest, "and I like it. Not as much as the cloud dust color we looked at earlier." She shrugs, pocketing the few samples we both agree on and roaming the edges of the room with a critical eye.

"This could be quite the costly renovation," she tells me with a conspiring grin.

I smirk back. "My thoughts exactly, which is why I need to go bug the Alpha about a certain paycheck I'm still owed."

Irina blinks owlishly back at me for a moment, the grin stalled on her face before it splits open into a wide smile. "Are you still going to make him pay you?"

"Obviously," I tell her with a fierce nod of my head. "I got the crystal back, didn't I?"

"Plus interest," she quips. We share a look at the thought of Luna, the naïve fairy who had been transported to our world through the crystal.

233

"Plus a headache," I amend.

"Maybe you can squeeze a few extra grand out of my brother for some kind of restitution for your fallen friend," she comments blithely.

I don't take her casual words too personally. They aren't meant to harm, but they bring up a familiar sadness. Irina's eyes and mind are already absorbed back on the task at hand as I wander to my suitcase near the end of the bed. Perhaps I had some photo on my laptop of the M and I together at some point? It wasn't the smartest thing to have on hand, being a thief and all—well, former thief—but exceptions could be made.

In my search, my hands catch upon a large envelope.

Pulling it out, my eyes alight with recognition: my last job proposal. I hadn't bothered to look it over too carefully with the Degas on my mind. The turnaround time hadn't seemed worth the effort for Mr. Vrana's needs. My fingers flick through the papers, idly taking in bits of information here and there about the item in want.

"Irina," I call calmly. She hums distractedly in response. "What's your favorite jewel?"

"Sapphire," she responds immediately, eyes darting suspiciously to me and the files in my hand. "Why?"

"What about amethyst?" Our gazes lock. Irina comes to my side and takes the paper I offer.

"Well, well, well," she murmurs, a devious tint to her voice, much like the one Ryatt owns. "It looks like you have one last job to complete. It looks like a big

234

job. No doubt you'll need the whole packs help for this one." We share a smile. I would indeed.

Continue reading for a sneak peek at
Wardens of Starlight

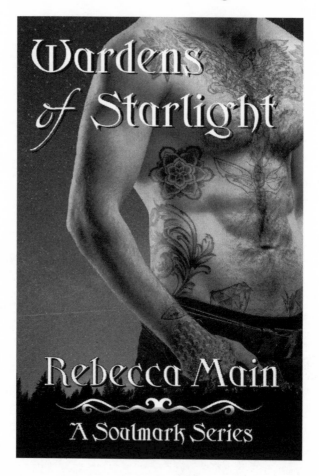

AMETHYST OF THE AZTECS
- Chapter 1 -

Relics line the walls of the atrium. Sacred
hammers and swords. Vinewood wands and staffs of
yew. Rings of amethyst, pearl, and pewter. Each with
their own unique history and power. Some forged by
gods of old. Others by those of new. I'm still learning
them all. The Wardens of Starlight seems to have an
almost endless supply.

Five months into my training as a Starlight
Warden and I have only just finished learning the
upper level of relics housed in the atrium. Five months
since I was reassigned from the Stellar Warriors and
sent here, to the Banks Facility. The Starlight Council
had called it a blessing. A righting of a wrong. I've lost
count of how many people told me that I was lucky to
be reassigned as a Starlight Warden. After all, among
my kind, women weren't seen as "well suited" for the
call of a Stellar Warrior. No. They are much better
suited for other trades. Trades such as Shadow Scouts
or Occult Scholars. Even a Weapons Master is better
suited for a woman than a position among the Stellar
Warriors. Or so everyone thought.

My fingers itch to toy with the butterfly knife hidden snuggly beneath my belt and sweater. Not a year ago, I had proven myself worthy of the elite group of warriors, yet one mistake and I had been kicked to the curb. Banished here instead.

Guilt coils heavily in my stomach.

It had been more than a mistake. It had been a tragedy. A massacre. And the blame for it could only be put on my shoulders. Maybe they'd been right to strip me of my warrior status after all.

"Are you listening, Callie?" Still lost in my thoughts, I let my head bob carelessly along. The triplets who occupy the atrium with me continue to speak, seemingly satisfied with my assurance. Then, an elbow smashes between my sixth and seventh rib.

"What was that for?" I wheeze, rubbing the offended bones. Nova sends me a smirk, her heavily lined eyes sparkling with mischief.

"Let's just say I had a gut feeling you weren't listening," she replies. I let out an unladylike snort.

The triplets are known for their "gut feelings" and uncanny ability to understand the power of the Borealis and the relics we keep safe. Most find their shared ability off-putting, but I didn't mind one bit.

"We're only trying to help you, Calliope," Noelle gently scolds. "Your final exam with the head warden is only a few weeks away."

"And she will not go easy on you," Naomi affirms, eyes large and doe-like. A wistful sigh falls past my lips. How unsurprising. Felicia Metzart is tougher than diamonds and smart as hell to boot. She expects no less than the absolute best from those under her tutelage, and I'm no exception.

The Starlight Wardens are the keepers of magical relics, but more importantly, they're the handlers of starlight. Only the Wardens are allowed to harness the mystical power sent forth from the sun—Borealis Matter—to infuse into our weapons and make them

238

unimaginably stronger. Only the Wardens know the vast secrets and knowledge of the world's hidden relics. Daggers that can cast a single un-sealable cut. Brooms that allow the rider to sift from place to place in the blink of an eye. Liquid gloves that can tame any flame. It is an honor to be among them.

Too bad my heart belongs to the warriors. Those who fight and kill the dark supernatural forces littering the earth.

"I know. I know," I finally lament, toying with the velvet cloth that drapes the altar we stand around. The rich fabric is out of place among the sleek white walls and glass display cases that houses the relics.

Noelle lets out a distinct *humph*. "Daydreaming about your time with the warriors won't do you any good now, Calliope." I send her an unimpressed look, enjoying a bit too much the way her cheeks color in embarrassment. "Your thoughts and talents are better put to use here than with them anyway. Don't you have your degree in astrophysics?"

"Yes," I confirm begrudgingly. *Not that I wanted to*, I think bitterly. Why JJ was allowed to go straight to his apprenticeship instead of having to run the ramparts of higher education is still a mystery to me. A niggling voice in my head croons a familiar tune; it's because he is our parents' favorite. I wouldn't be surprised if it's right. JJ is everyone's favorite. Including mine.

"Just because we don't risk life and limb to fight the monsters underneath the bed, doesn't mean we aren't cool," Nova teases. We share a smile.

"Oh, we're *cool* all right. We're stuffed in a glorified igloo up here in the middle of nowhere, Alaska. Reading books and dusting shelves all day. Oh lord," I groan, "we're librarians."

The three sisters wear matching expressions of disdain. "Librarians are cool," Naomi insists, fiddling with the glasses perched atop her head. My bluster

239

deserts me as I take in the slump of her shoulders. Of all the Stavok sisters, Naomi is the most sensitive.

"Librarians are cool," I concede.

"Hell yeah, they are!" Nova agrees. We share another smile. I spent most of my time with Nova. Whether studying dusty tomes or showing her how to handle my butterfly knife properly. We always seek each other out in the small fortress. Noelle rolls her eyes, smoothing a hand over the tight ponytail she typically sports as she fights down a smile. Nova continues, "Let's not forget we get access to the best shit. Did you know Felicia keeps the Baltic ivory harpoon head on her for 'safe keeping'? *At all times.* If that isn't a perk, I don't know what is."

"I do like that we get to wear our bracers all the time." The iron cuffs that adorn our wrist are etched with intricate spirals and notches. When activated by the wearer with a purposeful twist of the wrist, the etchings fill with a pale green luminescent light—the sacred power of the Borealis. The power increases both our strength and speed to almost supernatural proportions, but only the Wardens are permitted to wear the bracers at all times.

"What was that?" Naomi asks, mouth modestly agape. The conversation dies as our ears perk to catalog the faintest hint of movement or disturbance in the air. For a tense moment, my breath catches before Noelle shoots her sister an annoyed look and relaxes.

"Nothing, Naomi. You must be hearing things," she says. Naomi flushes, but her eyes dart nervously toward the sliding glass doors that lead into the atrium.

"What did you hear?" I ask.

Naomi flushes brighter and tugs the glasses off her face to clean them, a nervous habit of hers. "I just thought I heard a pop." While her face is downturned, I spare a look toward the other sisters. They wear

240

matching frowns, but Nova's seems to set itself deeper as her head cocks to the side.

"I don't hear anything," she finally says, stance relaxing. I mirror her movement. My shoulders relaxing from their stiff pose. I hadn't heard anything either, but the glass doors of the room are thick. Bulletproof-thick.

"Me either," Noelle agrees, gently patting Naomi on the shoulder. The youngest of the triplets flushes and places her glasses back upon her crown.

"Maybe something was dropped in the hallway?" Noelle opens her mouth to reply—no doubt to offer some half-hearted and thoughtless agreement—when a second *pop* occupies the moment. My gut clenches, and once more the atrium fills with roaring silence. The cool metal of my knife digs into my spine as I shift and walk toward the door.

"Where's Nathan?" *Where indeed?* The hallway is unusually empty, though protocol dictates at least one guard should be stationed at the end of the hall to patrol its length.

"Something isn't right," the triplets respond in unison. A tingling sensation flashes across my scalp and down my spine. An eager restlessness is quick to follow through my nerves and muscles.

Lights flash from overhead. They blink red in unison three times, pause, then repeat. That alarm sequence means only one thing.

"Wolves," I hiss. A sharp twist of my wrists outward and the bracers ignite. "Nova, get the dragon skin and balaclava. Noelle and Naomi, unlock the cases," I order stepping back from the doors.

"Who put you in charge?" Noelle gripes, though she does as she's told. I may not have seniority when it comes to the Starlight Wardens, but my fighting experience is far greater than the sisters'.

My eyes don't stray from the empty corridor. There is a fair chance the wolves won't make it this deep into

241

the facility. There is also a fair chance that Nathan is dead.

"Here." Nova presses the dragon skin armor into my arms, along with a modified balaclava. Our eyes meet for a split second just before the room goes dark.

Chances are the wolves have made it past the outer web, the first level of the facility, which means there's only one more floor between them and us.

I slip on the armor, which wears like a duster. It falls just above the knee with a slit in both the front and back to allow the wearer better movement. It fits almost as well as the bracers and protects better than the strongest Kevlar. By the time the generator sputters to life, I'm slipping the balaclava over my face and we can all see Nathan's body lying awkwardly at the end of the hallway, a pool of red ballooning around his head.

"What's your poison?" Nova asks. I glance at the sisters to see what they've chosen. Naomi holds a yew staff, Noelle a crossbow with silver darts, and Nova sports two souped-up .44 auto mag pistols. My fingers ache for the butterfly knife in my pants, but I gesture to the bone harpoon.

"Predictable," she taunts. I hold my hand out expectantly. The auxiliary lighting is nothing more than mediocre fluorescents, but they are enough. Minutes tick by as we wait impatiently for an attack, but the only thing to note is Nathan slowly bleeding out.

"Did you hear that?" Naomi asks.

No, I think, *just the sound of my heart in my ears.* Or the slight creak of the floor as Nova shifts restlessly from one foot to the other and the soft whisper of fabric as Noelle adjusts the crossbow in her hold. My eyes drift to Naomi. She is entirely at ease, her body loose, the staff griped only just enough in to keep it standing, eyes closed.

242

"What do you hear?" I breathe, tilting my gaze
back toward the glass doors. The triplets give pause.

"Currents," Naomi answers.

"Electricity," Noelle corrects softly. The fluorescent
lights begin to spasm, and one by one burn out.
Thankfully, our bracers provide more than enough
illumination.

"Fucking wolves," Nova mutters disgustedly as the
steady hum of electricity comes to an end all around
us. I find myself nodding in agreement. Why is it that
every beast and demon chooses to fight in the dark?

Figures emerge, eight in all, and approach the
doors.

"W.E.S.T. formation," I order softly. "Naomi, take
the south position. Noelle and Nova, flank middle.
Trigger point is me." The triplets move quickly and
silently to their places as I set myself firmly in the
lead point of our diamond shape. The door opens, and
a man with raven hair steps cautiously into the glow
of our bracers. He sports a lazy smile and a cut on his
brow.

"Now, now," he murmurs, "no need for any more
bloodshed. We're just here for a teensy, insignificant
piece of jewelry. A ring, as it would happen."
Something clicks, and a thin flashlight illuminates
more of the room. It scores the walls in pursuit of the
ring.

"No piece here is as you describe," Naomi responds
without inflection. The wolf turns a wayward glance
over my shoulder toward her before following the line
of the flashlight.

"I stand corrected," the man replies. I note the way
his gaze lingers on the south end of the room and
stiffen.

"Leave," I command. "You desecrate this sacred
place with your mere presence." The man shifts,
placing both feet wider apart as his hands form fists at
his side.

243

"That's not very nice," he comments, voice heavy with contempt.

"You're a mongrel," Noelle says.

"A beast," Naomi adds.

"A dog," Nova snarls. She fires at the floor. The bullet lodges itself an inch from his toe, but I'll give the wolf some credit for he doesn't spare it a flinch.

"Woof," he snarks back as something rolls between his legs. A cloud of smoke blooms from the rolling canister and into the heart of the atrium. It fills the room quickly—too quickly—and in seconds we are wreathed in a filmy white haze. Nova fires into the doorway. The sound of splintering glass and tearing flesh bear the brunt of her blind attack.

"Naomi! Fall back to the—"

"On it!" she replies before I can finish. If it's a ring they are after, the southeast section needs to be guarded.

A fist plants itself in my stomach before another thought can dart through my mind. I lurch backward, the force of the hit taking my breath and doubling me over. I clutch the harpoon tightly in my right hand and thrust it up and forward into my attacker's side. The figure in front of me lets out a throaty, masculine growl.

I yank the harpoon back, swinging it about to smack him across the face next, with the light of my bracers to guide me. He hits the ground a second later, and I feel a dark thrill of excitement rush through me. It feels almost sinisterly good to take down my opponents.

My breath sounds heavy in my ears, despite the commotion around me. For a brief second, scenarios and outcomes of the battle whir through my mind. There is no telling how many guards and Wardens have been taken out already on the upper levels, so I must assume the worst; we are all that's left to guard the relics. The bleak thoughts drive my fortitude and thirst of blood.

They'll retrieve their precious ring over my dead body.

I slash my harpoon to the left at the sound of feet. It catches on a body, and I ram it forward with relish. A raspy gasp follows as I yank the head out, then swing the harpoon in an arc to my right. It cuts through the thick smoke but nothing else. My feet shuffle backward, ears straining to hear the next oncoming threat. Another step back. I spin on the balls of my feet and swing the harpoon out to catch another enemy. Nothing.

Action blares behind me. Luminescent green streaks the smoke in jabs and thrusts. Some pause midair, strained and quivering, before forced left and right. There is no time to hesitate.

Instinct guides me as my other senses go into overdrive to compensate for my weakened sight. My harpoon strikes and latches on arms and legs, the press and pull of each motion dragging me closer and closer to the real fight. It feels as though the harpoon is an extension of my body. With each hit, my body surges and feints away, and I can't help the grim smile that lights upon my face as I take another punch to the gut. Then one to the face.

There it is again. The spike of adrenaline. The thirst for pain, whether to inflict or receive it, surges inside me without pause. Something inside me craves the fight. An irrational, adrenaline-laced rush I can't ignore. *A darkness inside me*, I think as I strike out with the blunt end of the harpoon to jab at the wolf behind me. *A darkness I have lost control of once before.*

Something smashes against a glass display case. Or somebody. The empty click of Nova's barrels sound, followed quickly by a startled cry that is unmistakably Naomi's. I favor the weaker sister and dart to Naomi

245

at the southeast end of the room, promptly tripping over a body and falling onto the glass-laden floor.

"Ouch! Watch it," a very feminine reprimand yelps from the ground. I suck in a deep breath and maneuver quickly into a crouch, diving forward into the body. She lets out a cry as we crash into the ground, squirming viscously and banging her hands against my chest as I fight to claim her wrists. "Get off you *bitch!*" she cries.

The sprinkler system activates above us, reacting to the smoke at long last. The woman beneath me sputters in indignation as the water doses us. Giving me the perfect opportunity to capture her hands. She struggles weakly against my hold. It's almost pathetic how weak she is against me. Almost too weak.

My breath catches in my throat, a sudden horrible realization stunning me.

"You're not a wolf," I pant, releasing her hands as if they burn.

The smoke is slowly dissipating around us, and I can make out the fright across her features. But only barely. I scamper off her, a thousand dreadful thoughts slashing through my mind, but one screams above all others: *not again*. Memories unleash themselves upon me with ruthless intent.

—A scared and broken girl clinging to my leg and the last remnants of her humanity. A plea for sanctuary tearing past her blood-soaked lips—

—A secret and betrayal. The strange nuance of hope that things will be all right—

—Human bodies torn to bits and pieces spilled across a chapel floor. The small child feasting on the steps of the altar. My mercy. My mistake—

—The blinding lights of the Auroral Bastille cast down upon me as I answered to the Councils accusations. Falling to my knees at their sentence and wondering how I could have been so wrong—

Something bashes into my back, knocking the air from my lungs. I fall forward. The raven-haired man helps the blonde up off the floor, pulling her into a dramatic kiss.

"Are you all right?" She nods, sparing me a wide-eyed glance. "Do you have it?" She nods again, and the man sounds off a shrill whistle.

No. A sharp burst of panic startles me into action, the feathering darkness pooling inside of me goading me back into the fight.

Stay low, my instincts tell me. *Use your environment to your advantage.* My harpoon lays somewhere behind me, but weapons coarse the ground. A jagged piece of glass is clutched in my hand in the next instant, and I slam it into the wolf's foot. He lets out a howl of rage, limping backward and dragging the girl with him.

I stagger to my feet as he rips the glass from his foot, my eyes frantically scanning the room to see most of the wolves retreating and the sisters regaining their ground. A knee surges into my line of vision too quick for me to process and knocks me solidly under the chin. Pain erupts inside my head as I crumple to the ground, my equilibrium further stolen by a heavy blow to my cheek. A final kick to my side leaves me grounded and watching in agony as the wolf and girl sprint away.

"Follow them!" I manage to order, watching as Nova and Noelle give chase through the darkened hallway. Sturdy arms wrap under mine to haul me up, tugging me forward as I take in a few strangled breaths.

"Are you all right?" Naomi asks. I nod and push her away, stalling at the doorway as a rogue idea swims into my head. We needed more bodies to take on the wolves, and I know just the place to get them.

"Stay behind and keep guard," I tell her, turning back around and running to the back of the room where a hidden panel leads to a passageway.

"Where are you going?"

"To fight fire with fire." I throw a quick grin over my shoulder as I pick up my harpoon and the bloodied shard of glass from the ground. Then, I'm running as fast as I can down the passageway to the back of the Banks.